SOMEBODY WANTS SOMEBODY DEAD

Boson Books by Phillip Gardner

Somebody Wants Somebody Dead
Someone to Crawl Back To
Necessary Evils

SOMEBODY WANTS SOMEBODY DEAD

by

~~Phillip Gardner~~

*For Tracy —
Really great to meet you, Tracy, and to eat and laugh really, really well — Best to you —
Phillip*

BOSON BOOKS
Raleigh

Published by **Boson Books**
An imprint of **C&M Online Media, Inc.**

© 2012 Phillip Gardner
All rights reserved.
http://phillipjgardner.com/

ISBN (ebook) 978-0-917990-66-3
ISBN (print) 978-0-917990-65-6

For information contact
C&M Online Media, Inc.
3905 Meadow Field Lane
Raleigh, NC 27606
Tel: (919) 233-8164
email: cm@cmonline.com
http://www.bosonbooks.com

Cover photo by Rick Cary
Cover design by Greg Fry
Author photo by Linda Erday

Contents

ACKNOWLEDGMENTS vii
THE LOOKING GAME 1
WHEN THE POLICE ARRIVED 9
TO BE SO DEAD HE SURE IS BIG 17
COLLECTIVE UNCONSCIOUS 23
WHAT I'M TRYING TO SAY IS 37
WHICH WAY YOU GOING 53
TWELVE TIPS FOR WRITING AN UNPUBLISHABLE STORY 63
SOMEBODY WANTS SOMEBODY DEAD 77
NEIGHBORHOOD WATCH 93
STEVIE BAKER'S SECRET SAUCE 107
DON JUAN'S WANTON LOVE 111
SPECK-NO'S BEACH 129

Phillip Gardner's collection of stories *Somebody Wants Somebody Dead* pretty much corners the market when it comes to people living on the wrong side of the law—which is usually the *right* side of the law in these locales—and taking matters into their own hands. Throw in a garbage collecting voyeur, an obese drowning victim, a Bicycle Man, and a whole knot of ne'er-do-wells and these fantastic stories will make you think, "My life's bad, but it ain't *this* bad," which is to say that Gardner's hit the mark in the tragi-comedy venue.

George Singleton—author of *The Half-Mammals of Dixie*

Acknowledgments

The author sincerely thanks the editors and staff members of the following journals where these stories originally appeared:

"Collective Unconscious." *Fifth Wednesday Journal*
4 (2009): 79-90.
http://www.fifthwednesdayjournal.org/

"Somebody Wants Somebody Dead." *Rainbow Curve* 6 (2005): 50-67.

"To Be So Dead He Sure Is Big." *The Bryant Review 11* (2010): 122-128.
http://bryantliteraryreview.org/

"The Looking Game." *Pisgah Review* 5:1 (2010): 9-16.
http://www.pisgahreview.com/

"Which Way You Goin'." Boson Books (1995). http://www.bosonbooks.com/

"Bingo! Or Twelve Tips for Writing an Unpublishable Story." *Louisiana Literature* 25.2 (2008) 69-86.
http://louisianaliterature.org

The Looking Game

The two men stood at the bumper of Taylor's truck cocooned in the dim blue light behind The Paradise Lounge. The broken asphalt around them was potted and puddled with rank summer rain. Mosquitoes hummed and swarmed.

Quelling the instinctive impulse to defend himself, Taylor, the older, forced his arms and his words to hang loosely as he measured the distance between himself and Stroud. "If you intend to take a swing at me," Taylor said, "this would be a good time to do it. Otherwise you run the risk of somebody seeing." The other man, Stroud, half Taylor's age and strapped with twice his muscle, hovered within arm's length, the younger man's body hard and bent as angle iron. He did not speak. "Time's runnin' out," Taylor said.

A rising torrent of anger produced an almost imperceptible quaking in the younger man's shoulders, like the stuttering second hand of a jammed clock. The blue halogen overhead carved twitching shadows in the sinew of his forearms and made cold dirty icecaps of Stroud's tight knuckles. A bead of sweat perched on his knotted jaw.

Taylor said, "You can probably take me—"

"I intend to," Stroud spat. Blood rushed inside the younger man's ears, and the mainspring of his oscillating rage brought his face so close to Taylor's that for a long second each inhaled the sour, hot breath of the other man's whiskey.

"I'm not questioning the outcome," Taylor said. "But I can promise you two things. First, I'm going to hurt you. You may be the one left standing, but I promise you I'll give you something to take with you. I am going to hurt you, boy. Second promise. There's no way you don't come away from this looking like a coward. You deck a man twice your age? Lots of glory there, huh Stroud? Don't think about it too long, boy." Stroud's chest and shoulders swelled to pitch. "Time's up," Taylor said. "That door is about to open. Somebody's gonna walk out. Somebody's gonna see. And everybody's gonna know. Do it."

"You first," the younger man hissed. "Break." Stroud lifted his twitching fists, his knuckles now raised white blisters. His face muscled up, the eyelids receding into nothingness, the veins swollen channels down the side of his neck. His clinched words hissed:

"Hit me," Stroud whispered. "Hit—"

Taylor's fist shot up from the side of his hip like the snap of a gunfighter's draw, the middle knuckle melding into the bridge of Stroud's nose with three inches still to give.

The younger man collapsed like a pricked water balloon. Blood slopped from his nose, a soft fountain flowing in every direction, pooling above his lip. And for a long moment his eyes were filled with distant childlike wonder. Taylor turned. "Piece of shit," he whispered as he walked back to his truck.

Young Stroud's pistol lived in the glove box of his pickup, and as Taylor shifted into first gear, he looked into his mirror expecting to see his daughter's husband taking aim in his direction, but instead he saw Stroud steadying himself against his truck, head down, both hands covering his bloody face.

***

They called it The Looking Game.

Phoebe invented it on their first fishing trip. She'd become restless, and Taylor said, "Just you and me can rest back on the blanket. I'll keep an eye on our lines. We'll look up at the sky and say what we see."

"Okay," she said. She tucked her small hands beneath the blonde hair. Her bare feet swayed in time to imaginary music. Taylor lay with one arm half-mooned above her, his fingertips covering her shoulder. After a time, Phoebe said, "I like this game."

"What do you like about it?" Taylor said.

"How it plays with my eyes," Phoebe said. "Makes them change."

"Let's take a look," Taylor said. And then he made a big deal of rising up on his elbow above her and studying the child's eyes like an eye doctor might. "They're still blue," Taylor said. "Let me know when they change to green."

Phoebe pressed her palm to his cheek, pushed softly. "Mama's eyes are green, silly," she said. "Mine are blue, like yours."

"Then what changes in your eyes?" Looking up at the summer clouds, Taylor eased back on the blanket.

"The pictures," Phoebe said. "I'm looking at the white clouds, the shapes they make." She lifted her hand. With her pointer, she traced the outline. "And then something happens and I'm looking at the patches of blue in the sky. My eyes go from the shape the clouds make to the shape the sky makes. That's what I mean."

"Ohhh," Taylor said. "So you're doin' the old eye dance?"

"Granddaddy!"

"That can't be," Taylor said.

"Can, too."

"I don't hear any dance music?"

"Granddaddy!" she said.

They lay studying the sky.

"I like it," Phoebe said.

"What?" Taylor said.

"The Looking Game," she said.

***

"Ohhh," Cora said. Taylor smelled beer on his daughter's breath. She turned, allowing the screen door to slam shut behind her, and drifted across the trailer's small living room. "I thought you were Stroud," she said to the room. "Lucky me."

"The porch light was on," Taylor said, opening the door, entering.

"My fault," Cora said. She picked up the remote on the counter and began going through the channels.

"Phoebe asleep?"

"Last time I looked she was. Something on TV you want to watch?" she said as she pressed the buttons.

"He's cheatin' on you, Cora."

"You want a beer?"

"No."

"Don't mind if I do." The father and daughter exchanged a long look. "You can stay or you can go," she said. "That's the policy around here." Cora opened the refrigerator. She spoke into it. "Stroud chose to go, which is okay by me. The two black eyes and a broken nose kinda took away his sense of humor." She turned and looked up at Taylor, her mock smile like a scar on the side of her face. "In that case, why don't you just sit down, Daddy? Make yourself right at home. Sure you won't have one?" she said with fake cheer, holding up her beer can like a trophy.

Taylor sat on the small sofa. When he saw Cora watching TV, he leaned forward and shut it off. "You're drinking too much," Taylor said.

As she glided toward the recliner, Cora said, "Runs in the family. So if that's what you're here to talk about, this is gonna be a very short, very dull conversation."

"Why?" Taylor said.

"I only cry when I'm sober?" she said. "How's that?"

"He's cheatin' on you. Why?"

"So?"

"So what do you think about that?"

"I don't know what I think." She drank.

Taylor motioned toward the beer she held. "What you do is what you think. You got a little girl in there."

"Who do you think you are?" she said in a lilt. "Comes to cheatin', I'd say you take the lifetime achievement prize." She looked away from him and said, "Like father like son-in-law, huh?" She looked at him again. "That high and mighty routine, it don't work for you, Daddy."

Taylor said, "I'm going to say what I have to say, and when I'm done, you're gonna say, 'I don't need this shit.' I know that. I understand that, okay? But if you ever did need me, if that little girl was ever in trouble and you didn't call me, I'd never forgive you for that. Never. There are necessary lies. And if you tell me necessary lies, I'll forgive you. Always. But if y'all are ever in danger or there's even a hint of trouble, don't you lie to me."

Cora tilted back her head, took a long pull on the beer. "I really don't need this shit," she said.

Taylor stood and made for the door. "No, what you don't need is another accidental bruise and a daddy like the one you got with me."

Cora's voice stopped him. "If a cheater cheats on a cheater is that still cheatin'?" Tears were tiptoeing down her cheeks.

"You seeing somebody?" Taylor said.

"I wouldn't put it that way."

"What way would you put it?"

"Maintenance man," she said. "That's how I'd put it."

"What are you telling me, Cora?"

"A necessary lie, Daddy. A necessary lie."

***

When the waitress set the plate of steaming pancakes in front of Phoebe, the child was looking out the window of the restaurant. Taylor tilted his coffee cup and the old woman poured more.

"What you looking at?" Taylor said. He drank from his cup.

"Monsters," Phoebe said.

"Clouds or sky?" Taylor said. The little girl's eyes were way out there. "Is it the clouds look like monsters or the sky that's shaped like 'em?"

"Both," Phoebe said.

He slid her plate closer. "You gonna eat?"

"Yes, sir," Phoebe said. Her hands rested in her lap.

"Here," Taylor said. He pulled the plate over and lifted his knife. "I'll cut 'em for you. What kind of syrup do you like?" When he looked up, Phoebe's eyes were out there again.

"What does *panic* mean?" Phoebe said. She was still looking.

He held the knife suspended before him. "To be real afraid," Taylor whispered. "Where did you learn that word?"

"I'm looking at it," the little girl said. She pointed. The restaurant sign was missing some letters. "It's The Pan_ak_ House," she said.

***

Taylor slowed and stopped at the four-way. Straight ahead, parked in front of the trailer, he could make out the outline of Stroud's truck. He signaled to turn.

"Where are we going, Granddaddy?"

"Riding," Taylor said.

"Riding where? Does mama know?"

"What?" Taylor said.

"That we're going riding?"

"I think she does."

"Where?"

"Around." Taylor craned to look past Phoebe, back at the trailer.

"Around what?" Phoebe said. "Around like a circle?"

"Riding is like fishing. You don't have to catch fish to go fishing. And you don't have to go anywhere to go riding."

"When we ride around, can we play The Looking Game?"

"Yes," Taylor said, glancing in his mirror.

"How do we play, riding around, I mean?" Phoebe said.

"I'll drive. You can't drive."

"Granddaddy!" Phoebe said. She smiled for the first time.

"The law forbids it," Taylor said.

"Granddaddy!" Phoebe gave Taylor's arm a soft tap. The tiny hand rested there. "How do we play?"

"I'll drive and you tell me where to turn. When you see something you want to look at, tell me, and I'll turn and you can look at it."

"That makes it The Looking Game?" Phoebe said.

"Yes," Taylor said.

For a few minutes, the girl instructed her grandfather to turn at every intersection to see barns and ponds and birds in the distance. But now she stared out like she was asleep with her eyes open. The low sun threw long shadows across the highway. When they passed through a thick growth of pines, the air was cool.

Taylor had driven around Cheraw and circled back through Bennettsville. "Want some ice cream?" he said.

Phoebe didn't take her eyes from the window. She spoke in a low, dreamy monotone: "I scream. You scream. We all scream for ice cream."

"We'll get us some," Taylor said. "We'll go back to Bennettsville." He turned onto a dirt drive beside the collapsing remains of a tobacco barn and shifted into reverse.

"There," Phoebe said, pointing toward an island of thin pines and scrub brush fifty yards into the empty field. "Let's go look, Granddaddy."

"What at?" Taylor said.

"The lights. Just now I saw something dancing in there."

"I don't hear any dance music," Taylor said. He smiled at her. But she didn't turn. He drove slowly down the narrow path.

"See?" she said. "Do you see them dancing?"

"Those are gravestones," Taylor said. "That light is the sun reflecting, jumping from one to another as we get closer."

"The dancing?"

"Yes."

He parked and they walked into the thicket. It was a family graveyard, most of its inhabitants Ervins or their kin. The saplings and briars were thick, their shadows like black welts and thunderclouds. Most of the headstones, many of them too worn to read, lay on the ground, vandalized.

"A lot of these fell over," Phoebe said.

"Yes," Taylor said.

"Did Grandmama's?"

"She's not here."

"Where is she?"

"Someplace else."

"Did she fall?" Phoebe said.

"No," Taylor said. "She didn't. Let's go."

"Can I have these?" Phoebe was holding faded purple plastic flowers. The vase had been shattered.

"Yes," Taylor said.

In the truck, he said, "We'll get some ice cream now."

"It's too late," Phoebe said. "It's past suppertime." She was studying the plastic flowers in her lap. "Mama, she wouldn't like it."

Still Taylor drove until darkness covered everything there was to see.

"I have to go home now," Phoebe said.

"I could call your mama if you want to spend the night at my house."

"Mama wouldn't like it."

***

From a quarter mile away, Taylor saw the pickup's quivering headlights. And when Stroud blew past them, the force dipped Taylor's truck a little to the right. A minute later, Taylor pulled onto the long muddy drive. Up ahead, he saw the trailer's front door slam shut and then the living room window shades fall. He parked, leaving the headlights on.

Phoebe pulled the door handle and the cab lit up. "Look, Granddaddy," Phoebe said. She had twisted the plastic graveyard flowers into a circle. She set the flowers on her head like a crown. "When I was three years old," she said, "I used to have a princess dress and a magic wand. I remember everything from when I was three years old."

The trailer's front door opened. Cora stood behind the screen wire, her right arm out in front of her like a traffic cop, her palm against the screen. Her other hand covered the side of her face.

"I got to go inside," Phoebe said. "Bye, Granddaddy."

Taylor laid his hand on her knee. "Tell me something else that you remember about when you were three." Cora turned. Taylor couldn't see the covered side of her face. "Then I'll tell your mama that you're spending the night with me. I'll get you some clean clothes. When we get home you can tell me all about when you were three."

Phoebe looked at her mother. "I don't think so, Granddaddy."

Cora backed away from the screen door.

"Okay. Tell me one thing you saw when you were three. Then I'll talk to your mama while you wait here."

"Like The Looking Game?"

"Yes," Taylor said. He glanced up again. Headlights flickered behind him in his mirror.

"Well," Phoebe said. "When I was a little girl, I could see stars that no one else could see. I wasn't pretending. I could really see them. And nobody could tell me I didn't see them, cause I did." Phoebe pushed open her door.

"Wait," Taylor said. "Tell me the rest."

Cora called from inside, "Phoebe?"

Phoebe let herself down from the truck. She lifted the crown of faded plastic flowers. "I'll leave these," she said, "here under the seat for riding around next time."

Taylor watched the predatory headlights in his mirror, then looked again at the trailer door. "There's a gun under there," Phoebe said.

"Don't touch it," Taylor said.

7

"What's it called?"

"Smith and Wesson."

In his rearview, Stroud's lights clicked high beam.

Phoebe spoke, now from the shadows. "That's Daddy," she said.

"Phoebe, get back in the truck."

"Mama, she won't like it."

"Get in."

"I can't see them now, Granddaddy. Those stars that only I could see? I used to could. But not now." She looked up at the dark, moonless sky.

"At my house," Taylor said, "the monsters, they're gone, Phoebe."

He couldn't see her face, her eyes. Her voice came from the darkness. "No, Granddaddy. I don't think so. They're just sleeping."

Taylor checked his mirror. In the truck cab behind him, the glove box light made black craters of Stroud's muscled face. Taylor felt for the pistol, but he didn't lift it. Instead, he extended his hand to the girl child.

Stroud called from the shadows behind the blinding headlights. "Taaaylor?"

"Go to your mama," her grandfather whispered. "Don't look, Phoebe," he said.

"Now, Taylor," Stroud demanded.

"You go on now," Taylor said to her.

Cora stood on the porch, her arms reaching. "Phoebe?" she called. "No, Stroud! Phoeeeebe!"

The old man looked back at Stroud's unsteady silhouette, the pistol wavering at his side. Phoebe was walking away.

"Go to your mama," he said. "And don't look back."

Phoebe turned, and Taylor saw her eyes as she looked up into the night then back to him in the dimly lit cab.

"Throw-down," Stroud slurred.

Taylor heard the unmistakable click, the cocking of a pistol's hammer. Not taking his eyes from the child, he felt for the pistol under his seat.

Cora sprang from the porch steps. "Oh, Jesus. Oh, Jesus," she said.

The child's face was tilted up to the black sky. When he felt the cold metal, he heard Phoebe speak.

"I can't see them now, Granddaddy," she said. She lifted her arm, as if she were making an offering. "Those stars that only I could see? I don't see them. All I see now, Granddaddy—is nothing."

When The Police Arrived

My aim—

I'm trying to be accurate here. The first time the police came—

By this I mean the first time the cops came as it relates to how everything ends. I was sitting in the backyard in my beach chair in my boxers with my BB rifle across my knees, resting on my lap. At first there were only two cops. You should know that these were Darlington police officers, dedicated small-town men, men from hard-working families, families with the best of intentions, families of limited means, church-going types who voted for George Bush. Twice. Families that didn't have health insurance.

Both officers wore blue, well-pressed uniforms as did the back-up cops. But these two—unlike the other four who charged toward me a couple of minutes later—these two wore glasses, thick ones, the kind of glasses prescribed to people who have lived most of their life with limited means and minimal health care.

When I heard the first cop's voice, I was calculating the distance between myself and the five mockingbirds in the fig tree. His name was Ed. We'd met a few years earlier, after my trip to the dentist's office. Ed said, "Mr. Case." He said it like the answer to a question.

I turned to look. The cops' thick lenses reflected the red summer sunset like four lasers. I instinctively reached for my BB gun.

The stereotype of small-town Southern cops is well known by our local peace officers, and most work hard to counter that redneck stereotype. Just for the record, they sound like newscasters as they draw their weapons and say, "S-i-r, release the rifle and slowly raise your hands, sir!"

When I turned to greet them and offer them a drink, they both shouted in rapid machine gun-like bursts. Their every other word was Sir. I had to smile, their pistols raised, both men moving in that familiar gorilla crouch; and my first thought was, This is just like COPS on TV. I tried to ask if they wanted a drink. But they wouldn't let me get a word in edgewise until Ed, the one with really bad teeth, had the cuffs on me. Ed clamped them so tight they didn't even make a clicking sound. I could feel my pulse against the cold steel.

On the other side of the fence between our yards, across the long sunlit glitter-green lawn, my new neighbors, the Sykeses, shaded their eyes. I could see their toe heads ticktock in time with the bad news from the neighborhood. This was not the first time they had called the cops. Maybe I'd been shouting.

Wearing only my boxers and a button-down, I didn't present much of a search challenge. Still, Ed lifted my shackled wrists and secured my jaw with the firmness most people associate with a dentist's moves. My cheek rested snuggly against my chest. When he steered me in the direction of the car with the blue flashing lights, the squirrels raised up on their thin hind legs, their perplexed faces tilted to one side. A few feet above them in the fig tree, the five mockingbirds I'd loaded my rifle for screeched I-told-you-so in spastic, lunatic joy.

I'm going for accuracy here.

I still think the cuffs were unnecessary. The chubby panting policeman who put them on me, Ed, the one with really bad breath, could see from five feet away that the rifle was a Daisy BB gun. I know this because the next day, after I'd sobered up, I set the rifle in my beach chair and took long backward strides to measure the distance from which I could clearly read the word Daisy. In The Great Gatsby, Daisy was married to Tom, who I think was a dentist, or was that McTeague? Ten feet was the distance. No, twelve. But I want to be on target, so I'm giving the cop with thick glasses and bad teeth and awful halitosis the benefit of the doubt. Which is a hell of a lot more than he gave me. Besides, he sort of knew me, from the other time he came to visit, following my discovery that my wife was sleeping with her high school boyfriend, a dentist in a bordering city.

The dentist didn't know that I knew. I made an appointment to have a tooth capped. When the dentist came in, we briefly discussed my putting a cap in his ass, and when I left his office he required emergency dental surgery. Soon after that, within an hour or so, to be exact, I met Ed, the cop with the spooky eyes and severe tooth decay at my front door. That first time he put the cuffs on me, he was a gentleman about it, a model of professionalism.

But my feeling the second time we met was different. Maybe he had finally found a dentist who would reconstruct his teeth on a payment plan a Darlington policeman could afford, and maybe after I administered my version of a root canal on the dentist, Ed's dreams of smiling for the camera died forever. I felt bad about that. When I asked him if he took vitamins—this was on the short walk from the arrest photo to the tank—he didn't answer. A proper level of vitamins can help prevent tooth decay, I told him. I was trying to be nice. Prevention, I insisted, was a purpose we both shared. "I'm in the insurance business!" I shouted as he walked away. The door shut behind him.

I don't know what became of my father's shotgun. I got the BB gun for my birthday. I was thirty-six. Bought it for myself. I had my reasons. That was the fourth summer after my wife and children left me. I have two boys and a girl. Or I did. I observe their lives through Facebook. It's my one-way observation post. Their teeth keep getting straighter and brighter.

That first summer I lost all the figs to the mockingbirds. There was nothing I could do about it. This was the third week of July in South Carolina and before the Sykeses moved in, at a time when possessing a handgun in your own backyard didn't trigger an alarm at the police station. When I got home from work it was too damned hot to drag the ladder out and pick what the birds hadn't vandalized. By the time the day cooled down and the bottom of my highball glass was five or six deep with ice cubes the color and shape of vanilla jellybeans, well, I'll put it this way: Falls are the number one cause of injury around the house. I've written the policies. I've taken the pictures.

I've discovered the remains.

Insurance is a funny business, people betting they will get hurt or killed, those of us in the industry betting not. It's all a gamble, all of it a crapshoot. Your payday comes either way.

It was my Dad, he taught high school English, who said I ought to go into the insurance business. He was a man with a sense of humor. Dad was fond of irony and wordplay. When I was a small child, he would take me on his lap and tell me stories about Rindecella and the Pee Little Thrigs. I'd laugh until I'd sometimes wet my pants. I liked the way he smelled too, which I know now was bourbon. When my mother moved out, I called to see how he was. He had this great laugh, my Dad. "Ohhhh," he said. "Everything is a fuster cluck." Then he laughed again.

My wife and I (I still call her my wife by habit) we're starting to develop better terms. I know this because when she refers to the dentist with the new front teeth—his name is William—she will say his name in a sort of Ole Shucks way and I imagine her tossing back her hair and sighing. Then she says, That William! and I sigh back and repeat, Yeah, That William, and this is our way of establishing a level playing field, one where I acknowledge that our marriage is over and that we can now discuss her terms for my seeing her children. This is a sign of progress.

She emailed me an old photograph last week of our youngest, Danny, taken when he was three. The email was titled: LIKE FATHER LIKE SON. In the picture Danny has lost his drawers and his little butt protrudes from his T-shirt. His head is turned back over his shoulder. The expression says he's been caught in the act. His mouth is open, partly in laughter, partly in protest, the sum of which is resignation. It's a look I've seen before. The thing is he's standing in the toilet, flushing it again and again.

My father's version of the Jesus story was titled, Easier Dead Than Son.

My wife has adjusted well, I have to give her that much. She's got her sense of humor back. If I were cynical and maladjusted, I'd say, "laughing gas" but I'm not, so I won't. She says she is fine. Everything is fine, she says. When I call, she answers the phone now. And when I ask how she is, she says fine. And when she asks me, I say fine. She says things are different. I wonder if they are little things.

If there were a next time, I'd do little things differently. The big things, the LIFE ALTERING EVENTS, would probably be the same. By the time you get to them, they've acquired a life of their own. The insurance business is based upon this probability. The little things, that's what I'd change.

For one, I'd buy my Dad vitamins, if things could be different. Not that he didn't eat right and get plenty of exercise. He did. And he had great teeth, perfect teeth. But—and I've done a lot of thinking about this—it seems there are small things a person can do that are, if you'll excuse the expression, like buying insurance. If you're in the business, you think that way. The point is, if I had bought my Dad vitamins, One-A-Day, and if he had gotten into the habit of taking them, you know, found some basis for order, something to organize his life around, something to count on, well things might have turned out differently. I know it's a small thing. But sometimes we can do small things to change a person's life, even save their life. Sometimes.

There are other things I'd do differently too, if there were a next time.

When the police arrived I was sitting in my beach chair in my boxers in the backyard with my Dad's fishing rod on my lap, resting across my knees, listening to Bruce Springsteen Live and enjoying another beverage. I always thought that was funny, Live Band. That's the brain of an insurance guy for you.

The goddamn mockingbirds were having a field day in what had once been my Garden of Eden fig tree. If you've never seen their work, they don't really eat the figs. They peck a small hole and drink the life out of them. The pulp hangs on, but there is no life inside. The whole damned tree was hung with what looked like testicles from the old folks' home. I can't tell you what it did to me, sitting outside in my beach chair looking up eight or ten feet and watching the mockingbirds destroy the figs. It really got to me. When the police arrived—the neighbors who moved down from Vermont or some goddamn place had called them. Theirs is an enormous three-story job, and I saw them huddled like frightened refugees on the upper landing as the cops, minus Ed, ushered me back to my chair. It was probably the cursing. Or the flailing about.

My wife's email said Lacy, that's our oldest, wanted two tickets to the Springsteen concert for her birthday. "Lacy wants to see The Boss," she wrote, "before he dies." I could see the smile on her face when she wrote that line. My father was a high school English teacher. In Death of a Salesman, the son, Biff, calls his father, the boss. The double barrel shotgun Hemingway blew his brains out with was manufactured by a company named Boss. Funny, the things you remember.

It was probably the cursing. Or my futile, exhausting attempt to whip the mockingbirds back to hell. The fishing rod, or what was left of it, was mine, a gift from my Dad. With all the breath I had left, I shouted to the cops that it was my goddamn yard, and my goddamn tree, and my goddamn figs, and my goddamn fishing rod, and to get the hell away from me. I usually don't talk like that. I sounded like a stranger. I apologized.

After I sat down, I offered the cops, there were four or five by this time, a drink. The next morning I crammed the remains of my fishing rod into my neighbors' trash can, along with four pounds of frozen shrimp. The galvanized handle was already so hot that it burned my fingers. I think the fumes made the lid tremble. You should have seen the flies.

I don't know what happened to my father's shotgun. I don't want to know.

My Dad had been good at sports, baseball, basketball, and, when he was older, hunting and fishing. He was as good as they get with a Browning automatic and a covey of quail or a spinning rod and a top water plug. He'd tell you where he was going to put it, and he'd put it there. His aim was true. When I was a boy, I saw him pinch a lure with the fingers of his left hand, slowly draw it back, bending the rod, sight-in, and slingshot a Devil's Horse under brush and limbs where the big bass cooled, places that couldn't be reached any other way. He was good. The sportswriters at the city newspaper asked Dad to take them fishing. That's how good he was. Once he took me.

At the end of the summer, the large fig leaves yellow and fall, and after a rain they leave a brown spoor around the skeleton of the tree.

The summer he took me fishing I was twelve. I didn't walk a step that summer, ran every one. Ours was a gravel drive, and by July 4th the bottoms of my feet were so tough I could run, even slide, on the fiery rocks. Then, I never seemed to be running from, but always running to—or running for running's sake. I sort of couldn't help it. When Mom sent me to the store, I'd ask her to time me.

"Time?"

"Yes," my father says.

In early spring, he'd put new line on his spinning reels. That meant removing the old and replacing it with new eight-pound test, then pulling out and reeling in the new line a couple of times to straighten it so as to avoid potential kinks and knots.

"Get a hold," he says.

"Now?"

"Yes."

We'd eaten supper, but the exhaust fan from the kitchen still blew the smells of fried chicken and hot biscuits out into the evening air. The field beside our house was freshly plowed. You could smell the dirt, black as coal dust, the rich aromatic dirt smell all around; that soft, damp soil, and the smell of my mother's cooking. The cool darkness was settling in and everything you could see was soft in shape, soft in color. Dad made a loop in the line and secured it to the small black Mitchell spool. He turned the handle and the bail clicked over. Then he cranked the handle so fast that the moon-curved bail was at once a silver circle, and the spool fattened with the quiet accumulation of clear, clean line.

When the spool was full, he cut the line, and without speaking, handed it to me. I couldn't see his face, only the outline of its features against the dying light of the cool spring horizon. But I felt his warm hand as he wrapped the line over my palm and closed my fingers around it. I feel it now. Then he stepped back, behind me. Gone now.

"It's getting dark," I whisper.

"Run hard while there's still time," he says.

"Tell me when the line's about to run out?"

"You're way out there. Will you hear me?"

I raised my fist triumphantly and held the line high like a torch, waiting. I was just a boy, twelve years old. The last summer of my father's life.

I waited for the click of the bail's opening like a sprinter awaits the starter's gun. Then it happened. My bare feet pounded the soft black dirt between the rows and the only sounds were of my breathing and the rapid thud of my still tender feet in the ever-expanding darkness. I ran until I felt the fire in my lungs, and I closed my eyes then as I do now. My arms pumped, whipping the line, knowing that the end had to come soon, not knowing when, not knowing then that everything had to

come to an end, and I feared the sudden shock in my hand when it did. But I couldn't stop. Not then. But that was then. And that was that.
   And now this is this.

To Be So Dead He Sure Is Big

Donnie Swank said, "He sure was big."

"Especially to be so dead," Ex-Ray said.

"Six-foot-eight, maybe two-fifty?"

"That's before he was dead."

"I pity the dead," Donnie said.

"I pity the pallbearers," Ex-Ray said. He stood on the bank of the Great Pee Dee River, mulching his hairy chin. "He was a big-un to start with. As swole as he is, we'll need a front-end loader to get him ashore. How many men do you figger it'll take to get him from the hearse to the grave?"

"When I volunteered to fight fires, I didn't sign on for this," Donnie said.

"If you got some lighter fluid, I can solve that dilemma for you, Donnie. Be like settin' a cruise ship on fire. Damn, look at the size of him. How long you reckon he's been in the water?"

"I'd say for at least seventy-five or eighty pounds," Donnie said.

"I'd call him a clay color. What color would you call him, Donnie?"

"I'd call him clay."

"Clay it is," Ex-Ray said. "What do you suppose explains why Clay's still in one piece? There's catfish that would have him limb by limb."

Donnie lit a cigarette while he considered Ex-Ray's question. "They're not biting."

Ex-Ray was looking up at the sky. "Who's not biting?" he said.

"The catfish," Donnie said. "They must not be biting."

"Just goes to show," Ex-Ray said.

"What?" Donnie said.

"You don't have to catch fish to go fishing," Ex-Ray said.

"Are you talking about Clay here, or are you talking about the catfish?" Donnie said.

"There aren't any catfish. You said yourself they weren't biting." Ex-Ray said.

"Lucky for old Clay here, huh?"

"Clay's luck run out."

"Damn," Donnie said. "For as big as he is he sure is dead."

"Look at the flies," Ex-Ray said. "I hate a damned fly. With some people it's mosquitoes, with some it's gnats. Me, it's flies. Flies from Hell. Especially those big fat green ones there. Clay's head's swarming like a beehive from Hell, ain't it? How about you, Donnie? What is it with you?"

"Snakes," Donnie said.

"Let's keep it to the insect population. What is it, flies, mosquitoes, or gnats?"

"I'd say spiders."

"Spiders, that's good."

"No, maybe fleas."

"I can stand a flea over a fly any day, especially those green blowflies. Look, I think they're making a nest in Clay's ear."

"Ticks," Donnie said.

"Oh, hell yeah," Ex-Ray said. "If Clay here was red, as swole as he is, he could be a giant tick."

"Would we call him Tick?" Donnie said.

"No, we'd naturally call him Red."

Donnie said, "If we don't get him out of there soon, I'm not sure he's gonna come out in one piece."

"You could grab one arm, me the other. We might at least get him on shore."

"If we do that," Donnie said, "then what? Think of the flies."

"Damn, Donnie. I wish you hadn't said that. I hate a fly."

"We need a plan for getting him out of the water and into something, like the back of a pickup or something. We must exercise economy of effort," Donnie said.

"Economy of effort?" Ex-Ray said. "Where'd you learn that, Jeopardy?"

"I made it up," Donnie said.

"Bullshit."

Donnie and Ex-Ray studied Clay's circumstances. Ex-Ray wagged his head from side to side. He said, "Look at the size of that hand."

"Big as a flipper," Donnie said. "You'd think he'd be tired of waving bye-bye by now."

"Just the motion of the water," Ex-Ray said.

"You got no imagination," Donnie said. "None. Nilch. Nada."

"What is that, German? Or did you just make it up in that fertile imagination of yours?"

"I'll tell you who got no imagination," Donnie said.

"Clay," Ex-Ray said.

"Damn right," Donnie said.

"Those green blowflies, they can smell a dead man from like five miles away. I saw it on the Discovery Channel."

"I don't get it," Donnie said.

"Me neither," Ex-Ray said. "Nature is a mystery to me."

"No," Donnie said. "I mean, why, if you despise flies, would you watch them on TV?"

"The whole show wasn't about flies, Donnie, just a little piece of it."

"Same difference," Donnie said. "When they started talking about flies, why didn't you turn it to the Braves game?"

"If the Braves had been playing, what makes you think I would have been watching the Discovery Channel in the first place?"

"Think Clay would have been baseball?" Donnie said.

"I'd say football."

"Or basketball, big as he is."

"I'll wager one thing," Ex-Ray said.

"What's that?" Donnie said.

"Swimming wasn't his sport."

"You should be careful about making fun of the dead, Ex-Ray."

"I'm not making fun, I'm stating a fact."

"It's a good thing he's face down, don't you think?" Donnie said.

"Be funnier if he was face up," Ex-Ray said.

"You should be ashamed of yourself."

"Gettin' a little holy there, aren't you, Donnie?"

"We should give Clay a little dignity."

"You first," Ex-Ray said.

"What?" Donnie said.

"Fire away, Reverend. Say a few words for the recently departed."

"When the wind shifts, I'd say not so recently," Donnie said.

"You know what you are?" Ex-Ray said. "You're a hypocrite."

"I just don't want to turn him over," Donnie said. "You don't know what the other side looks like."

"If he could talk, old Clay would tell us what the other side—that would be death—looks like," Ex-Ray said.

"Do you think it matters if you're drunk when you die?" Donnie said.

"I never thought about it," Ex-Ray said.

"Do you think Clay was drunk when he died?"

"I'd say so."

"Me, too. Got drunk, fell out of the boat. Couldn't swim, or swim drunk."

"They don't make life preservers that big, do they?"

"You mean for as big as he is, or as big as he was?"

"As big as he was."

"I don't know."

"Don't matter now. Damn he's a big one. If the bank wasn't so steep, we could back the truck up and drag him out with the winch."

"In ten years of fire fighting," Donnie said, "we haven't used that winch once. I don't even know if it works or not."

"This would be the time," Ex-Ray said.

"Does it take you longer to die the bigger you are?" Donnie said.

"That's a good question. If so, this boy's been dying for a week."

"Smells like it," Donnie said.

"Which of your senses is strongest," Ex-Ray said. "Seeing, hearing, smelling, touching or tasting?"

"I'd have to say smelling," Donnie said. "That's why I became a fireman. I can smell a fire five miles away."

"For me, it's seeing."

"That why the flies get to you so bad?"

"Maybe so."

"They say when you get older, your sight goes."

"Same true for smell?"

"I don't know. Why do you ask?"

"Cause so many old people smell bad," Ex-Ray said. "Maybe they don't smell each other."

"You mean maybe they don't smell bad on purpose."

"Yeah. Like Clay here."

Donnie said, "Do you think he did it on purpose?"

"People have their own reasons for getting drunk. Or no reason at all."

"I mean do you think maybe he killed himself?"

"Possible," Ex-Ray said. "But I'd do it another way."

"Drowning does seem like a awful way to die."

"Slow," Ex-Ray said. "And as it turns out for Clay, messy. Real messy."

"But the fast way is really messy," Donnie said. "Besides, if Clay didn't want his family to know that he was killing himself, this would be the way, don't you think?"

"Hanging. Now that's the choice of one stupid man. First it's slow and painful. And second it's messy. And third, ain't no doubt but that you killed yourself. If I ever commit suicide, Donnie, don't let me hang myself," Ex-Ray said. "I'll find some other way."

"Our choices here—" Donnie said.

"Some other way," Ex-Ray said.

"What are you talking about?" Donnie said, reaching for another cigarette, looking over at Ex-Ray. But Ex-Ray, who was studying the empty sky, didn't answer.

Then Ex-Ray said, "Bob."

"What?" Donnie said.

"He looks more like a Bob than a Clay."

"What are you talking about?"

"That motion, up and down, up and down."

"Why would Bob kill himself? Why would anybody?" Donnie said.

"Couldn't take it, I'd guess."

"He should of believed in Jesus." Donnie looked up at the sky. Ex-Ray studied his shoes and pulled at his chin. Finally Donnie said, "Flies don't make nests."

"What the hell are you talking about," Ex-Ray said.

"A few minutes ago, you said those flies were making a nest in Bob's ear."

"Flies lay eggs. That's what they're doing in Bob's ear."

Donnie said, "Why did you try to change your name, Ex-Ray?"

"I wanted to start over, you know? I did the crime, I did the time. I just wanted to start over."

"But you didn't start over, Ex-Ray. Ain't but one beginning, one ending."

"It's what happens in between the two that keeps me awake at night," Ex-Ray said.

"Why didn't you go somewhere where not everybody knew you?"

"Nowhere to go."

"Maybe Bob Clay here had nowhere to go."

"I've been there," Ex-Ray said. "I've been there. That's why I'm here."

"But everybody knew you were Ray. Even after you changed you name, you were still Ray."

"You got to start somewhere, you know? Changing your name, that's a start."

"But it didn't work. You just went from being Ray to Ex-Ray."

"Sometimes you just feel desperate, you know?"

"Yes," Donnie said.

"He sure is big to be so dead, ain't he, Donnie?"

"He sure is, Ex-Ray. He sure is."

Collective Unconscious

What the garbage guy didn't know was that the husband and the wife sometimes had "sex dates." The two were strangers to him, so there was no way he could have known. He would have laughed had he heard this piece of private language the man and his wife shared, but it would not have been a ha-ha sort of laugh. The two were the NPR-ish sort, what the garbage man called snobs. He knew they were snobs after one glance into their garbage, at the art and business magazine titles he couldn't pronounce. These people meant nothing to him. They were just a garbage stop on his normal day. What they chose to call their sex events never crossed his mind.

Another thing the garbage man didn't know was that the wife insisted her husband accompany her to the health club they belonged to. She wanted the husband to see the effect of her tight abs and expensive breasts on the other men at the club. This was shorthand for she was considering leaving him.

Fridays, the garbage man observed the couple as they returned from their health club. Snatching and dumping trash bins in their cul-de-sac with the power lift, he would watch as the woman descended from the Lexus SUV wearing her thin silver leotard that showed everything and that reflected the morning sunlight like snake skin. He'd take her in like a snapshot, snap, and carry that snapshot inside his head late into the night.

Neither the wife nor the husband even noticed him. They often spoke of the poor as they sipped their wine, but they rarely saw any poor people.

***

Wine was always included in their sex dates. At first, it was the wine and only the wine. But that was early in their relationship, at a time when the other accountants at his firm teased the man, calling his wife-to-be a gold digger. She would sometimes arrive unannounced at his office two minutes before an important meeting, just long enough to show him her new Brazilian wax job. In those days, his wine and money were all it took for her. It was also during the getting-to-know-you Brazilian period that the man discovered his wife's love for expensive French stockings. Before the breast enhancement surgery, all she'd had were those legs, which were her pride.

After a time, wine wasn't enough—or maybe "enough" wine was too much.

***

The man was always discovering things about his wife. At first he loved this. Later he hated it.

When he first sensed that she was slipping away from him, he began surprising her with rare wine, expensive art and exotic stockings. They would sip Dom Perignon then she would excuse herself with a fetching smile and, at her dressing table, apply red lipstick before coiling sinuously into a red silk gown. She'd slither into the expensive black stockings and stand before the mirror in four-inch heels. She never thought of her husband as she watched the woman in the mirror rehearse for their sex date. Sometimes it would be a famous celebrity she thought of, other times a man she'd shared an elevator with or another she'd studied subversively at a traffic light. But never her husband, who made money but was soft all over and whose skin was sensitive to sunlight. When she returned, he'd pour champagne, she'd light a candle, and when she had finished her wine and felt like it, they would have a sex date.

***

Inside their trash bin, the garbage man saw the packages the stockings came in, the photo insert of a tall dark woman with long legs in the sheer black stockings. He carried that picture and his snapshots of the wife inside his head late into the night.

***

What the husband feared was that he was losing his wife, and though he didn't love her, he didn't want to lose her. He was an accountant. Losing her didn't seem to add up.

***

What the husband didn't know was that his wife had had an affair with a younger man at the gallery where she volunteered. The husband didn't suspect, at least not the younger man, who was a painter and whose slight build and gentle manner the husband misinterpreted. The husband was a good accountant, good at making money and managing office politics, but he wasn't good at anything else and he knew it. So to keep his wife, he avoided thinking too much and concentrated on balancing the books.

Still, she grew tired of him, for the thing she had demanded of him, his submissiveness, she came to despise in him. The thing she most feared, a man who would not bow to her, was the thing she most desired. The sum of her fears and desires created an appetite, a hunger in her. So the young painter made reckless love to her on those mornings she arrived early or at the lunch hour or, quickly, at the end of the day. Their sex was nothing like a sex date. They never undressed. Frenetic clawing and biting spoke to a need in her.

At the end of the day after exacting her price upon the young painter, the wife locked the gallery doors and, inside the Lexus, attended to her makeup as she opened her cell phone to tell her husband she was on her way home.

Soon she owned the young painter. Still her hunger followed her like a shadow.

***

For a time, when she and her husband had sex dates, the wife could close her eyes and think of the young painter. But that time passed.

***

What the wife didn't know was that her husband often experienced powerful moments of insecurity and self-doubt. At the accounting firm he was routinely interrupted and regularly informed of important decisions made in meetings to which he had not been invited. A few of the much younger men at the firm made jokes in his presence that were clearly at his expense but always cloaked in terms too vague to justify reprisal. When he made a suggestion, one of the young accountants would look at another young accountant and make a remark about "Pop" culture, which was their chosen euphemism of denigration.

He overheard two young women, the two that all the accountants wanted to make, refer to him as "gross." He realized they could smell his need.

***

What nobody realized was that the husband had begun to slowly boil.

***

What his parole officer told the garbage man was that everything would be okay so long as there was some anger management happening in the garbage man's life. The garbage man insisted he didn't have a problem with anger. What he had a problem with was somebody—anybody—

telling him what to do. That included his parole officer, but he didn't say that. Instead, what he said was, "No problem."

***

What both the husband and the wife knew but that the garbage man could not have known was that a new man had appeared at the health club. The new man was not gentle. His face had the angular and iconic look of chiseled granite. Sometimes he would wipe the sweat from his face with a towel and look at the wife as if he could ravage her right there, with everybody watching. At these moments the wife could not hide her desire to be ravaged. It was all over her. On these mornings, she would leave the gym hungry for the new man. Other mornings, the new man would ignore her. When he did this, the husband noticed that the new man and his wife reached for the same towel or arrived at the water fountain at the same time. The wife and the husband, whom the new man made invisible, drove home from the fitness club in silence.

The gifts, cards, and stockings he brought home to her remained in their plastic wrapping in the bottom of her dresser.

***

In violation of the wife's desires, the new man at the gym did not appear for two weeks. Perhaps, she thought, he had purposefully altered his schedule, that maybe he'd begun coming to the gym in the afternoons. Perhaps he was speaking to her in code. Perhaps this change would present the perfect opportunity for the perfect thing. In a roundabout way she asked the Spanish-speaking female attendant at the club about the new man, but the attendant said that sort of information was confidential. The wife made the young brown woman cry. The husband, who had begun showering at the fitness club, sensed some connection between the crying attendant and his wife, who sat erect in the Lexus, waiting impatiently for him to drive them home in silence.

This was the third week in March, when everything was covered in yellow pine pollen. In the early morning light, you could see it in the air, this cloud of yellow. It got into your eyes and sweat turned your skin a rank green. It was everywhere, even on the Lexus.

Standing at the rear of the stinking truck, the garbage man pulled the hydraulic lever that lifted the green trash bin and dumped its contents. The garbage man's eyes were on the Lexus, not on the trash, as the March wind, thick with yellow pollen that worked on you like mustard gas, lifted two plastic grocery bags like balloons and sent them tumbling in the direction of the Lexus. The garbage man paid no attention to the wind-filled bags because he was taking mental snapshots of the woman stepping out of the car. Snap. The silver jogging jacket dangled from her hand. Her skintight black top was sleeveless and nicely scooped in front.

When the woman saw the plastic bags floating toward her, her abundant chest inflated with indignation. She stepped on one of the bags and bent to pick it up. Snap. The second bag puffed and skirted erratically, like a kite without a tail. The woman slammed her silver jogging jacket on the grass in the direction of her husband, who stood in front of the Lexus SUV watching. She snatched the second plastic bag from the yellow air, gave her husband a commanding look, then turned and marched toward the garbage man.

The garbage man didn't see the woman's face because he was watching her breasts, taking a mental picture to carry with him into the night.

"Trash," the woman said pressing the plastic bags into his smelly thick rubber gloves. Even with the air thick with yellow pollen and the garbage truck three feet away, he could smell her. Even with the pine pollen covering everything, he could smell her gym sweat. "Trash?" she shouted again as if the garbage man didn't speak English. The yellow light was like glitter on the skintight black material that covered her very large breasts. "You wouldn't know trash if you saw it," she sneered.

The garbage man tilted his head slightly and looked at her dead-on. For an instant, a bright current flashed from his eyes to hers.

Snap.

He brought his gloved index finger to his eye, then drew a line from his eye to hers, a line that seemed to hang in the yellow air between them. The woman turned to walk away. The garbage man began to laugh.

"Peekaboooo," he said in a little boy's voice.

She looked back at him. The pine pollen worked her eyes like hot sand. He saw the yellow flames in her eyes now. Still he laughed, but not ha-ha.

As she approached her husband, she gave him a look that said Pick up my damned jacket. His eyes went down to the silver jacket on the yellow grass and back up to hers; then he turned and started for the door.

The garbage man had stopped laughing, but she could feel him looking at her. When she bent to retrieve her jacket, she glanced to see that he was sizing up her backside. At the open door to their safe suburban house she looked at him one last time. The garbage man had taken off the smelly rubber gloves. He leaned against the rear of the garbage truck with his arms across his chest. When she reached to shut the door, he was laughing again.

***

That night, the garbage man lay in his bed imagining the puzzle parts he hadn't seen. When he had her all put together, he drew a deep breath. And when he resurrected her scent, his eyes slowly shut.

That night, the wife dreamed of the garbage man. In the dream, the guy was not a garbage man but she knew it was he—the man who had thrown her scorn back at her. She never saw his face. He wore thick leather gloves. The wife sat on the rear of his motorcycle at a hundred miles an hour, her thighs contracting around him, the deafening blast of the engine with its hot penetrating undulations rising from the pounding pistons beneath her. The pulsations surging up her muscled thighs and through her body like shimmering currents of summer heat off the fresh black asphalt of her dream. And of course the fear, the exhilarating fear. She shut her eyes and pressed her breasts into his back. In the rushing darkness she lifted her hand to his chiseled face, to the coarse black grit of his beard. When she found his thick lips, they parted, and her fingers sank into the hot, wet mouth. And at that moment, she woke, and to her breathless relief her husband had not yet come to bed.

That night, the husband sat downstairs drinking single-malt Scotch and watching an adult movie on high definition DVD, a movie purchased to spice up their sex dates. But now he watched alone, imagining that he was included in the strangers' date.

***

What the garbage man didn't know was that now the husband refused to go to the health club three times a week. He'd had enough, he told her.

Certain that the new man would suddenly reappear and set into motion the perfect thing, the wife attended the club alone. But the new man never showed. On her drive home she cursed the new man though she didn't know him, not even his name. She felt abandoned, jilted, and angry.

She parked the Lexus in the drive and started for the door of their secure suburban home. She refused to look at the garbage man standing at the curb. But he watched her, every inch of her, for there were still pieces of her puzzle he hadn't put together. He debated calling to her: Where's the hubby? But he thought better of it; he'd just look. He liked the way she looked, but he didn't like her. She was nothing, nothing but the pictures he carried with him late into the night, to do with as he pleased. She was garbage to him.

At the door she could not resist looking back at the street, at the garbage man looking at her.

He smiled. Snap.

"Fuck. You," she said.

***

The garbage man had spent his life bending the rules. Too often he'd bent them until they snapped. There was something magical for him in that infinitesimal space between bending and snapping, a fascination that charmed him the way the dance of flames infatuated others.

The following Friday, he sifted through their garbage, separating out all the plastic grocery bags. After he'd emptied the other contents, he dropped the plastic bags back inside. That same afternoon, in a storeroom in the gallery, the wife brushed against a metal picture frame and ripped her pantyhose. She peeled down the stockings the way she had with the young painter and stuffed them inside her purse. Later, she remembered them when she felt for her car keys. At home she tossed the stockings into the trash bin. She saw the plastic grocery bags, and she knew.

The next week, the garbage man left a third of their garbage in the container. The wife complained, but the husband reminded her that they never filled the bin in a week's time. What difference did it make? She said that the garbage man had a job to do and that he should do his job. But the husband didn't want to listen. By obligation the night before, he had joined the other accountants at a strip club. One of the young guys, one who made thinly veiled jokes about Pop Culture, was getting married. At the end of the night, the husband got stuck with the tab. He didn't want to hear about anybody's job or what they should do.

***

What the wife didn't know was that for the garbage man there was no quitting once it had begun. He became blind to the caution signs, deaf to the warnings. She wanted nothing to do with the garbage man. The sight of him disgusted her. She feared him. So she parked the car in the garage and entered the house through the side door. But her fear was mixed with something else. She began counting down to Fridays, and when she came home from the gym a few minutes early, she stood naked behind the blinds waiting for the garbage man to show.

***

Each week he emptied less garbage from their bin. She clenched her fists until her palms were red and her knuckles white as blisters, and she cursed him until she felt breathless and lightheaded.

***

One day when she stopped at a traffic light on her drive to the gallery, a garbage truck passed through the intersection. A moment later a Harley rumbled to a stop beside her. The first two pieces of an elaborate puzzle? She couldn't see the man's face.

At lunchtime, she dialed the number for the Sanitation Department. She thought the call would end it. She complained. The complaint was registered. Still she could not stop thinking about the garbage man. At the traffic light on her drive home, she suddenly remembered the motorcycle man, and the pieces of her dream came back to her fully.

Her husband had already poured a single-malt Scotch when she walked in. She poured herself a glass of wine. Then another. For the first time in months, they had a sex date.

***

The next week, she watched through the upstairs window shades as the garbage truck passed their garbage bin without stopping.

"You better do something about this," she said to her husband.

"What does it matter," he said. "It's only half full." Then, remembering their sex date, he tried to kiss her to take the edge off. She pressed her hand into his soft, doughy chest.

"Next week you are going to stand right there," she pointed out the window at the curb, "and you are going to take care of this." He forced his thin lips upon hers. "NO," she shouted. And for an instant he thought she was going to say he was gross. But she didn't. "You're such a pussy," she said. She left him standing in the kitchen. He took the stair steps two at a time. He had some things to say to her. But she had locked the bathroom door.

At her desk in the gallery, she dialed the Sanitation Department. "If you don't want me to make you cry, you'd better put me through to your supervisor," she said.

The garbage bin was empty when she got home that afternoon. But she didn't feel anything like satisfaction. If anything, she felt her insides winding tighter and tighter. She could hardly wait.

***

What the husband didn't know was that something had passed between his wife and the garbage man that day she slammed her jogging jacket to the ground and instructed him to pick it up. Nor did he know as he parked his Lexus that his wife had taken the day off from the gallery to clean their garage. Nor did he know that cleaning was not her motive. Her only aim was to fill the green bin so that her husband would have to confront the garbage man the next morning.

What the husband did know was that political wheels had been turning at the accounting firm and that he would soon be working for the young man who referred to him as Pop Culture and who had left him holding the tab for tit dances.

"What are you doing?" he said when he saw his wife working inside their garage. He had to speak loudly because of the blaring mower, which was operated by a small brown man with a name neither the man nor his wife tried to pronounce.

"What does it look like?" she shouted back, brushing a yellow cloud of hair from her eyes. She wore a man's thick gloves and stood beside the brimming container with her arms folded under her plentiful breasts.

"What you got in there?" he said, looking down into the green cart. "That's not trash." He reached for a paintbrush in its unopened package. She pushed his hand away.

"You wouldn't know trash if you saw it," she hissed. She said it with the exact inflection of You're such a pussy.

"Wanna bet?" he said. He looked at her and laughed. But not ha-ha.

That night he drank single-malt Scotch downstairs. And when he was drunk and thought she was asleep, he turned the volume up full blast on their expensive in-home surround-sound entertainment system, and the animal cries of strangers on sex dates roared up the stairs and into their bedroom, where the wife lay awake but with her eyes shut tight.

The next morning, he was not completely sober when he left earlier than usual for work. The man told himself he'd have a word of prayer with his very young boss-to-be, a little man-to-man chat before the day officially began. That same morning, the wife did not go to the health club. Instead, she wrapped her nakedness in a soft red robe and wheeled the garbage to the curb.

Then as an afterthought, she rushed into their entertainment room and gathered her husband's adult DVDs and dropped them on top of the other trash and shut the lid. She thought she was sending her husband a message about the sex dates they wouldn't be having. Then she took the stairs up to their bedroom and waited at the window.

When she saw the garbage truck and heard its shrill brakes take hold, the wife felt a dull nausea arise. She'd been sure that the truck would not stop, that it would pass like a ghost ship. She had even rehearsed her call to the head of the Sanitation Department, having chosen the exact words. She would make her demand and the Sanitation boss would take action. But instead, the truck stopped and the garbage man swung from its rear and bounded forward, arms wide, head tossed back, like a dancer singing in the rain. His lips were shaped for whistling, or maybe a crude kiss. Smiling broadly, the garbage man glanced up the street, she felt certain, for the Lexus. As if to music, he flipped up the cart lid with one gloved hand, caught it with the other. He paused, held the pose, his face shielded from her. The wife bent forward, near the window. The loose robe fell open. Her prescient blood surged. Drawing a slow deep breath, she felt her breasts swell. Her lashes touched the narrow wooden blinds. She waited.

The cart lid descended as slowly as a theater curtain, and his face surfaced as if from murky dark green water.

His unblinking eyes slowly ratcheted up to the window.

The wife recoiled, and synchronously, the garbage man too fell back. Her eyes remained fixed upon him. As if to rhapsodic violins, he slowly bent backward offering himself to her, his arms rising and extending like black wings, his broad chest thrust forward like charred regal armor. His hollow-eyed countenance reflected the brilliant morning sunlight like polished black marble. Green larvae-laden blowflies hovered in the thick air around him.

Nothing moved. Then a grand, triumphant smile bloomed upon his face, shattering its glistening darkness into webbed cracks, the sweat there emanating fissures of yellow sunlight. An electric charge ran through him. His gloved hand shot up in a victorious Nazi salute.

Then she saw them, the adult DVDs that he held up like a trophy.

The garbage man tucked one smelly gloved hand against his ribs and bowed deeply to the full garbage cart, rose with a little skip step, and leapt onto the narrow shelf at the rear of the truck. And just as the driver pressed in the clutch and jammed the transmission into gear, the garbage man howled like a wolf.

***

What the garbage man didn't know was that when he arrived for work on Monday morning he would be fired from his job as a garbage man. He would not be surprised though. He knew plenty about getting fired. It was something he'd been good at all his life. Getting fired never crossed his radar. Instead, he sat on his broken sofa and drank cheap wine from a paper cup, watching professional sex-daters having sex dates on his secondhand TV. He was watching them, but he wasn't thinking of them. What he was thinking of, what consumed his thoughts, was his picture of the wife watching these sex-daters on the screen. He pictured her watching and imagined her eyes and the look on her face as if she sat beside him on the broken sofa, the two of them devouring the sex upon the screen. A kind of animal intimacy for her stirred inside him, and when it became too much he had to close his eyes.

***

What the garbage man's parole officer didn't know was that when the garbage man said, "No problem," he meant no problem for the garbage man, not the parole officer. The parole officer thought that No problem meant that the garbage man had some anger management happening in his life, that the garbage man would do as the parole officer said and find another job pronto. The garbage man insisted he didn't have a problem with anger. What he had a problem with was the parole officer telling him what to do. But he didn't say that.

***

What the wife didn't know was that her husband had cut the legs from under the younger man who was now his boss at the firm. The husband was able to do this because he was a very good accountant. It was the only thing he was good at. What she didn't know was that a very good accountant with a taste for blood could tear out a young man's liver and eat it while it was steaming. The young boss man, though recently married, had retained his appetite for a large-breasted woman at the firm, one who considered the husband gross. When the husband came to his young boss's office for a little man-to-man, he sat down across from the other man's big desk. He told his young boss he was there to talk about balancing the books and about the leverage of a retainer. He used the word "retainer" euphemistically throughout the brief conversation, and when the accountant husband walked out of the other man's office, he owned the other man. That afternoon, without his wife's permission, he bought an expensive motorcycle, a Harley.

***

What neither the man nor his wife knew was that if you work as a garbage man, you get to know your way around. You learn how to get from here to there. You learn all the short cuts. You learn the ropes. The two could probably have figured those things out; they both held advanced degrees and were NPR types. But they just never thought about what a person who collected garbage might learn on the job. They never even thought of people who collected garbage as having automobiles or a second change of clothes. They never thought that someone might have a reason to follow them through their day or to put together the predictable patterns that were their lives. They didn't know that, for some, taking a puzzle apart could be more gratifying than putting the pieces together.

The man and his wife only feared people they knew: the harm that the young man at the firm would attempt upon the husband, what the testimony of the young painter could do to the wife in divorce court. But neither feared the damage a stranger might do to one or both of them, depending on how and when certain things came together like pieces of a puzzle. Although they were NPR types, imagination was not their strong suit.

What the garbage man knew from his years in the state penitentiary, what he knew firsthand that the wife and the husband lacked imagination for, was that the devil you know is child's play compared to the devil you don't.

And so after the man and his wife dressed in their expensive new Harley leather and straddled the engine of the powerful motorcycle, neither thought to notice the battered old pickup three or four cars behind them, the one missing its front bumper. Or the man behind the sunglasses wearing the baseball cap and drinking cheap wine from a paper cup, the soiled man beside them in the ragged truck who smiled in deference to them at the stoplight. Neither put two and two together. They thought only of the fury and philter, the motorcycle, their sex dates.

***

What the man and his wife didn't know was that the garbage man was all about short cuts and ropes and how to get from here to there. The garbage man was a puzzle with some parts missing, but imagination was not one of those missing parts. He knew about ropes and stockings, about cutting things, about getting from here to there.

It never occurred to the happy couple that the man who had collected their garbage might be a man with time on his hands. And to the very end they would never understand that when he lectured them about puzzles and ropes and stockings and cutting from here to there he would be recording snapshots, snap, snap, to carry inside his head. And not even in their last moments, when the garbage man had to close his eyes, would the two understand that when he said, "No problem," he meant no problem for the garbage man.

What I'm Trying To Say Is

It's what you learn *after* you know it all that matters.

This is my ex-wife, Amanda. And what you're seeing is that look on her face, the expression that says, Go ahead and say it; I know you're dying to say it; just go ahead. I can't wait for you to say it. I dare you. Play that card, sucker.

"I was just kidding," I said. "You think I'd spend our tax return on a dead dog?"

"When people say, 'Just kidding,' they usually aren't." She tilted her head slightly, like a poker player with a winning hand.

"What do you want me to say, then? That I wasn't kidding? That what you want?"

"What I want, Kevin, is for you to tell the truth for a change."

What I wanted to say was, One ounce of truth and you'd require CPR. That was before she left me. What I said was, "What kind of truth are you wanting to hear?" which isn't much better.

"You see, that's my point."

"How about we use that tax money to buy me a Seeing Eye dog."

"See, you're doing it again. See what you're doing?"

I closed my eyes. Picture me doing my best Ray Charles impression. It was funny then.

"You're impossible," she said. "Sometimes I hate your guts." She folded her arms and turned so that she spoke to the wall. "I really do," she whispered, a slight sniffle in her voice.

"You hate my guts?"

"Yes."

"My guts?"

"All of them."

"Okay, then." I said.

She turned. One side of her face slid up to form a bad imitation of a smile. "Then we can use the money to buy the tanning bed?"

"No. About my guts. I don't much like them either. Buying a tanning bed is about the stupidest idea I've ever heard." It just came out of my mouth. Just like that.

And now Amanda turned another notch toward the wall. She drew up her shoulders like a diving bird pulls in its wings, and she began the slight trembling to communicate she was crying but holding it all inside, keeping all that suffering from entering the world. Dying, you know, from the inside out.

"I was just kidding," I said. The trembling became a quake. "Okay, okay," I said.

She drew in a fierce breath, creating a kind of gurgling in her nostrils.

"Okay? I can have the tanning bed?" she said in a whisper.

"Okay, I'm going to tell you the truth about something."

"You're doing it again," she said. "You're doing it again."

"First things first. Truth," I said. "You'll like this one. It'll make you feel better. A truth you've never heard. This one's gonna change the course of our conversation. You'll laugh."

"For once you'll let me have my way?"

We were still married you have to understand, and what I wanted to say was, WHAT? You always get your way.

What I said was: "Truth: There are no ducks in Jesus stories. Undisputable truth."

And now she was boo-hooing.

***

Lovers don't "fall apart" so much as they engineer their departures.

Amanda and I had been devising the demolition of our marriage without knowing it. We both should have seen the breakup coming, but we just shut our eyes to it all. At least I did. Picture me doing my best Stevie Wonder.

It's not quite as funny now.

It's not like either of us wanted the divorce. But once the erosion started, it carved its own path. You see, it's not the breaking of a heart that you have to train your eye for; it's the signs of its being chipped away. Erosion. The little things. The tiny cracks and fissures are what you have to look for. Those things that you can't really put your finger on, those moments you don't have eyes or words for. Fact is, I don't even know if there is a name for what I'm trying to say. If you've got the word, I'll pay you for it.

Names, I've learned, have a way of creating their own truths.

Manda. Her name-name is Amanda. Amanda, it's like music: the repetition, the ah, ah, ah sound. Many a man would fall for that, including me. I loved my wife, still do. But after the sugar melted away from our marriage, Amanda cut her hair like a pageboy's and demanded that I call her Manda, as in mandate and mandatory. I don't do mandatory.

To make matters worse, when we separated, my wife moved in with her mother, Mabel, the Queen of Mandatory. Names. Words. What you wish you had or hadn't said.

Mabel is country. Here's what I mean. She calls herself May-bell. Now there's a red flag. So during the time when I'm trying to make amends for the tanning bed, my wife instructs me to call her Mander. How much love would that require? I ask you. Mander? Just the sound of it conjures up the image of a tailed amphibian, a reptile.

***

You may not even like your wife anymore, her name may make you think of lizards, but after a split there's going to come a time when you want some of her sex.

Maybe you don't think so. But if you've been married for a long time and have had even the minimum number of sexual encounters with your wife, what you'll come to know is that given the right set of circumstances and the guarantee that you'd never be found out, you'd consider having sex with a warm watermelon. The sexual urge will make you howl at the moon. What I'm saying is that following a split in a long marriage the acquisition of sex becomes a central feature of your thoughts, which in turn shapes the words that come out of your mouth, especially after a beer or two.

***

By this time, I had acquired my own barstool at The Paradise Lounge.

"I'm as horny as a three-balled tom cat," I said to The Bicycle Man. I raised my hand so that George Miles would bring me another beer.

"There's a reason it's called the world's oldest profession," the old man said. The Bicycle Man had some other name, I'm sure, but we knew him only as The Bicycle Man. The rumor was that he had been a college English teacher before his drinking and driving practices reduced him to two wheels. That was a long time ago. Now he owned a secondhand bicycle shop on the same block as Social Services and The Lord's Shelter, where they give medical care and food and the love of Jesus to those in need.

"I never paid for sex," I said.

"I'd say living with three testicles is a heavy price," the Bicycle Man said.

George Miles brought my beer. I motioned for him to bring one for The Bicycle Man. The old man's face was unbearable to look at. A crust like dried sea salt covered his thick brow and formed scabby red patches on his neck and cheeks. His ears were filled with burrs and deposits like frozen road sludge. "You're gonna pay either way," he said. "Always." The professor in him was still there. You could see it in his gestures, hear it in his voice. "You must consider what's at stake."

"That kind of sex, it's not the same," I said.

"What's not the same about it? You can call it what you want, but sex with a woman you don't love? What difference does it make what you call it? Because you are gonna pay."

At that moment I thought of Amanda's breasts. They weren't show quality, I mean like in a sex magazine or anything. After all, they were real. Over fifteen years, I'd seen them a thousand times, fallen asleep cuddling one of them for most of those years. In my current condition, I'd have sold my truck for just a peek.

"I reckon if you want to fool yourself about what paying is and is not, try The Thunderbird Lounge," the old man said. The Thunderbird was near the interstate and had a dance floor.

"I have," I said. I drank.

"And?"

"Nothing but a roomful of hot flashes, mustaches, and mean," I said.

"I rest my case," the old man said. He drank, leaving white foam above his lip. "If I'm gonna pay, it's not going to be for that." He lifted his glass. "George," The Bicycle Man called. "Bring a phone."

George Miles brought a round of beer.

"You got to call her," George said to me. "You got to call your wife."

"I can't do that," I said.

"You must," the old man said.

"No."

"Then you better save your pennies for some sex," the Bicycle Man said. "You have to do it for yourself. The sexual drive is the force of life talking to you, and you'd better listen. Could be a matter of life or death, if not literally certainly figuratively. It's a big secret. The death takes many forms. For starters, listen to your own words, then count your genitals. See what I mean?" He waited for me to show that I understood, which I didn't at the time. I wish you could have been there. When the old guy saw that I wasn't following his lecture, he did a brilliant Ray Charles impression. Then he opened his eyes and leaned in close. I won't comment on the odor of his breath. "It's not popular to say so," he said confidentially, "but all you have to do is look to nature. The sexual act? It's the only thing we're good for. If women could have kids without us, we wouldn't be here. It's as simple and sorry as that. Call her. Beg her for some sex." He slid the phone over.

"I wish I could," I said. The words sounded like the truth coming out. We both drank.

The old man studied my face as if it was an algebra problem. "I'm gonna tell you a story," The Bicycle Man said, releasing a deep sigh. "It's called, 'Story for My Grandson'."

"What?" George Miles shouted. "You? I just can't picture you as somebody's daddy."

"If your mama was truthful—" The Bicycle Man began. Everybody laughed and George covered his ears. Then he continued, "Why not Story for My Son, George? Nephew? or Army Buddy? Why Grandson?" The old professor let the question hang for a second. "No. Let's make it great, great, great—"

"I've lost count," George said.

"Math never was your strength, my son." Everybody laughed harder.

"Because why?" George said.

"Ask your mother," The Bicycle Man said. And now everybody's face was glowing.

"No. No," George begged. He held up his hand to say, I give. "Okay. Why for your great, great, great—" Everybody was laughing. The whole place was laughing.

"That stu-stu-stutter comes from his mama's side!" the old man shouted over the laughter. "Because—" He gave us a minute to catch our breath. Then he continued with great deliberateness. "Because this is a story about what's never gonna change." George was setting cold beers on the bar.

"On me, Bo," he whispered, nodding at the beers. George drew a deep breath, then bent forward, resting his elbows and cradling his chin in his hands. His face was still flushed. The old man drank. Later, he would be drunk, but not now. Later, he'd sing a Wobblers' song called We Got Racin' Cars.

He began. "So, it's her birthday, or your anniversary, or a day when you've smashed up the car again."

"You'd know a plenty about that last part," George said.

"Shut up," the old man said. He turned away from George with the inflated carriage of a drama star and spoke to me. "Now you and me, Kevin? What are we gonna do when we get to the Hallmark Store? I'll tell you what we're gonna do. We're gonna sweat. And we're gonna spend twenty dollars and we're gonna pray that's enough. We're gonna search for the words—somebody else's words—to say what we don't have a name for, to say, Please promise that you won't stop giving me some sex, cause if you do I'll feel worthless and die a death worse than fate."

"Whuut?" George said.

"Silence," The Bicycle Man said. He lifted his beer and drew in a deep breath. "Now suppose she forgets your birthday—it could happen—or she smashes up the car for the twelfth time. What's she gonna do?" He raised his glass and inventoried the faces on either side of him along the bar, looking from one to another, gathering in his students' attention. Then he set down his glass. "She's gonna do what we want her to do, that's what. She's gonna lift her shirt, exposing her naked breasts and say, "Heeeeere's your Birthday cards!" He looked at me again. "And you and me, we are as happy as we're ever going to be. You have to call her. Beg if you have to."

"I can't. I spent our tax refund. On two bird dog puppies. They both got run over before the check cleared."

The Bicycle Man gave me a look that scared me a little. "Call her," he said.

I reached for the phone.

Mabel, Amanda's mother, picked up. "Hell-oh," she said.

"Let me speak to Amanda."

"Who?"

"Manda," I said.

"No one by that name resides at this number."

"Mander."

"May I ask whose calling?"

"Cut the shit, Mabel," I said.

"Fuck-ya very muuuch," she said in a singsong voice and hung up.

I pushed the phone away and dug into my pocket to pay my tab. The Bicycle Man and the others had intentionally started new conversations to give me a little privacy. The name for it is "Male Code." Time to go, I thought. Otherwise I'd be staggering out the door at closing time, without even a bicycle, singing that Wobblers' song, If You Ain't Here After What I'm Here After, You'll Be Here After I'm Gone.

The Bicycle Man called to me before I could make the door. "Maybe it's more than her sex you're missing. Maybe you love her. Call her."

I reached for the door.

"May the force be with you!" George shouted.

"Shut up," I said.

I entered the McDonald's drive-thru and parked in the Walgreen's lot beside Amanda's Honda. I ate my cheeseburger and fries and waited for her to get off work at eight. It had been months with no sex, and I felt like a teenager. I couldn't take my eyes from the automatic door at the front of the drugstore.

At a little after eight, my heart muscles were doing jumping jacks. The early evening light had that soft yellow easy-on-the eyes summer glow to it. And when the magic door opened and delivered Amanda, both my heart and my sexual organ leapt. She was one pretty woman. I opened the door to my truck, and my buddy and I stood waiting.

Amanda held her cell phone to her ear. She didn't look up until she was maybe fifteen feet from me. She stopped cold.

"Hey Amanda," I said. "I came to talk to you."

She pointed at her phone. "Thanks, but I'm already talking." She dug into her purse then inserted the key in the door lock.

"Don't do me like this, Amanda. I came to talk to you."

She spoke into the phone: "Wait. Wait. Do you hear that?" She held the phone at arm's length and did a three-sixty. She brought the phone back to her ear. "That's the sound of somebody who gives a shit." Then she closed her cell, got into her car, and cranked it. I stood at her window. She dropped the transmission into drive.

I tapped on the window. "Amanda," I said. "Please." She looked away. "Please." When she turned, the tears were streaming down.

I said, "What I'm trying to say is—."

She lowered the window and looked up at me with a meanness that I don't have a name for. Her voice sounded like it was coming from a pair of vice grips. "And the Lord said, 'If it looooks like a duck, and if it waaaalks like a duck, and if it quaccccks like a duck—.'"

Then she drove off.

Weeks passed.

I prayed that time would heal.

Both my heart and my loins grew heavy. Then heavier. My mind and my eyes played tricks on me. I would be in the Food Lion buying frozen TV dinners when some busty woman would lean low over the freezer—and you have to know this was no beauty queen, nowhere near Amanda's league in looks. I'd suddenly feel a stirring down there, a kind of caged feeling. I'd let my mind go while I stood in the checkout line. I'd imagine following Ms. X out to her car and into her bedroom, see her begin undressing. Then, no matter what, Ms. X became Amanda, and I was going nuts to have sex with my wife. I couldn't even imagine another woman.

Later, I'd remember what The Bicycle Man had said about abstinence, and I'd think, This is the first sign of the slow death. Then one day, a word spoken by the Bicycle Man came to me: *atrophy*. I looked it up in the dictionary. I didn't sleep much that night.

Amanda refused to see me. Said she'd take out a restraining order. I'd park on the far side of the lot, on the Food Lion side, and watch her materialize and walk from the magic electric door to her car. She had a great tan.

I began to beg.

***

Begging gives comfort and aid to erosion.

I went to the Hallmark Store with a pencil and a yellow tablet. I took notes. I called her cell. I left yellow messages on the windshield of her Honda.

Begging became the pattern of my life. I wore Amanda down.

Then she agreed to have dinner with me. "Dinner," she said. "A very short dinner."

We met at an Italian place called Runts in Hartsville because Amanda insisted we go someplace we hadn't gone "when we were married," she said. I was dressed an hour ahead of time. Creased slacks, shined shoes. I sat on the very edge of the sofa, patted my foot to no music, and watched the first inning of the Braves game. But I can't tell you one thing about it. I don't even know who they were playing.

When I saw her enter the restaurant, I floated from my chair. I don't have words to tell you. I know it sounds corny, but she was all I saw, like when everything disappears but her, like that time years ago when she walked up the aisle. What I'm trying to say is there was no place else on earth I wanted to be. What I'm trying to say is I felt I was in the middle of a chick flick. What I'm trying to say is that what I was feeling was not about sex.

I held her chair. She didn't speak.

"Your hair, it's longer."

"Than what?" she said.

"You look really great."

She did. She wore a scooped red dress I'd never seen. Maybe she'd lost a few pounds, too. Her soft skin was the color of honey. The effect made me rock like a mentally challenged person.

"Let's eat," she said.

The waitress must have been listening. She was at our table before I could open my mouth. She laid down menus.

"Hiii," she said. "I'm Donner?"

"Donna?" I said.

"I'll be takin' care a'ya. What can I bring you two to drink?"

"Two beers," I said. Amanda held a small mirror and refreshed her red lipstick. I wanted to dive across the table.

"Two Buuud Liiites?"

I couldn't take my eyes from my wife. Amanda nodded. Donna was gone.

She pressed her lips together and dropped her compact into her purse. She spoke before she looked up. "I was thinking about you the other day—"

"I think about you all the time."

"I was reading this article in a magazine while I was waiting for my tanning appointment?"

"God, you look great."

"Truly?"

"Hell, yeah."

"And there was this woman—"

"What?"

"In the magazine story. And she bought this dog, you see. She wanted a dog. The article didn't say so, but I got the feeling her husband didn't want her to have the dog."

I pressed my hands together under my chin in an attitude of prayer and leaned in.

"All she wanted was a dog. A dog is not too much to ask. My feeling is that her husband thought the dog was a stupid idea. The story didn't say so, but you get the feeling that the husband thought his wife's getting a dog was the stupidest thing in the world."

"I'll buy you a dog," I said.

"You're not listening," Amanda said.

Our beers arrived. The waitress tilted back and rested her notepad against her breasts. I looked again at Amanda's low cut dress.

"Are y'all ready, or do you need a little more tiiime?" she said.

"Give us a minute," I said. "We're really not in a hurry."

"Okay," she said.

"What's good here," Amanda said, "and quick."

"I always reckermend the lazzanyer," she said. She lowered the pad and started away.

"Thank you, Donner," Amanda said.

As we lifted our beer glasses, my wife looked around the restaurant as if she might spot somebody she'd like to talk to. I resumed my position of prayer. "What happened?" I said.

"What happened? That's why we're here isn't it? You tell me. I wish I knew."

"I mean in the story. The dog story."

"Ohhh, the dog story, huh?" We both lifted our glasses. "She found a man—"

"She found another man?"

"What?"

"The woman."

"She found a man selling dogs."

"Not her husband."

"What are you talking about?"

"I'm sorry. Keep going."

"In the newspaper, she found a man who was selling dogs."

"I thought you said it was a magazine."

"The woman in the magazine searched the newspaper for a dog."

"What kind of dog?"

"How the hell do I know, I'm not looking for a goddamn dog."

"So what happened?"

"You're wearing me out, Kevin. The food hasn't even gotten here and I'm exhausted. I need to take a nap."

"So, what happened?"

"With the dog?"

"The dog. The woman. Her husband."

"Her husband's not really in the article I read. I was telling you what I think. But you're never too interested in what I think."

"Then tell me about the woman and the dog."

"You see? You see!?"

Ray Charles was my first thought, but I put it aside.

"I promise to shut up if you'll finish your story."

"You never kept a promise in your life."

I bit my tongue. Then we both finished off our beers. Donna was very attentive. "Two more Buuud Liiites?" she said.

"Yes," Amanda said. "Our food?"

"Food'll be right up."

"Thank you, Donner," my wife said.

I gave it a minute to let everything settle down then did that move kids learn in elementary school: I zipped my lips shut.

Amanda took a deep exhausted breath. "So despite her husband's thinking that buying a dog is the stupidest thing in the world, the woman buys the dog."

You'd think our server was wearing roller-skates. Our beers appeared. Then as Amanda sips hers, looking all around for an exit sign, looking at anything but me, the world feels like it stops. All I hear is silence. Somebody's turned the air conditioning down to zero.

Finally I said, "Did the dog make the woman happy?"

"What are you talking about," Amanda said, speaking to somebody over my shoulder.

"The woman in the story, was she happy after she got the dog? Did that make things good again?"

Amanda looked away, drew in a deep breath, and then looked right at me. "The dog died."

"What?"

"No sooner had the woman gotten attached to the dog, and the dog up and died."

"What did she do?"

"She didn't know what to do. She was at her wits' end. She put the dog in the freezer, thinking that after enough time she'd bury it."

"That's it?"

"No, stupid, the dog died. Don't you get it, the dog died!"

"Did she ever bury the dog?"

"No." Amanda's eyes were tearing up again.

"Is he still in the freezer?"

"The dog was a girl. It was a girl dog that died."

"What about the woman?"

"She lived."

"What did she do with the dead girl dog in the freezer?"

"She took it back to the man who sold it to her."

"Get her money back?"

"You don't know shit. You never have. This is hopeless. She didn't want money."

"Why did she take the dog back?"

"She beat the man—with the frozen dog. She left him for dead."

"The dog?"

"The man."

"No shit?"

"When she got home, she beat her husband with the dog, too."

"Did she kill her husband too?"

"No. The dog had begun to thaw out by that time."

Our food came. Lots of red sauce. We didn't talk during the meal. Amanda didn't want dessert. Neither did I. Our server brought back my VISA card.

"Thank you, Donna," I said.

"Donner."

"Excuse me?"

"Like the reindeer," she said: "Donner."

Outside at her car, I said to Amanda, "Will you see me again?"

"You're a blind man."

"Will you?"

"You quack me up," she said. "You really do." Then she drove away.

***

The next day, The Bicycle Man died. Heart attack.

At his funeral, I was told that he had been in the middle of rebuilding a vintage Schwinn when he keeled over. His casket reminded me of a tanning bed.

George Miles, the Paradise Lounge bartender, bought a wood burning kit and etched "The Bicycle Man" on his barstool. We missed him. Together we all sang We Got Racin' Cars. Everybody had a Bicycle Man story. I caught myself wondering how long the old man had lived without sex. Couldn't help wondering if his advice to me—and his fate—had come from his own bitter experience of living without.

One night after leaving The Paradise Lounge, I dreamed that I was in school again, sitting at my desk. I was holding a Bible. There was a duck in front of me, sitting on my desk, facing me. The duck was very patient, quacking and nodding, thinking—the duck was—that I was understanding the translation of the Bible in Duck. It was one of those dreams like you can't find your car, and by the end of it the duck had become a frozen duck.

***

A few beers sometimes open you up, help you find words for things that otherwise have no words. I'd found the courage to call my wife, to open up to her, to tell her how much I really loved her, how much I missed her.

"I don't think there's anything you can do for me," she said.

"Amanda?" I wanted to finish my sentence but out of nowhere I lost my voice. My voice came out like a throaty cry. "Don't you just sometimes need a little human touch? Don't you need that?"

And now I heard the little lurches and the deep intake of air and the gurgling in her nostrils.

***

Terrence Gangly is a city cop. When we see him in uniform, we call him Terrence. But when he comes to The Paradise Lounge late Saturday nights we call him T. Sometimes after George Miles locks the doors, T will sit and have a beer with us.

At one o'clock on a Sunday morning, Terrence showed up with a bicycle. George unlocked the doors. We watched as T rolled it in. The bike was vintage, like the one the Wicked Witch rides in The Wizard of Oz. Big wide seat and all.

"This is what's left," T said to George. "What's left of The Bicycle Man's bicycle shop. They wiped him out."

We all circled round the cop and the bike. Its frame was freshly painted bright red, the fenders white enamel. Against the bright white and red, the new oiled chain was the color of cracked coal. T said, "The Bicycle Man's crew took them, every one. They broke into the old man's shop, wiped him out. Just got this one back tonight, after an arrest. I think he'd want it kept here, George."

"Whuut?" George said.

"The girls. The Bicycle Man's girls." George and I exchanged looks. "The hookers. You didn't know about the old man's girls? The last week or two, they stole all the bikes from his shop."

Suddenly, I remembered. I'd seen them.

"I thought they were Jehovah's Witnesses," I said.

"Deals on Wheels," T said.

"Maybe we could mount it on the wall," George said. He turned and pointed.

***

I bought Amanda a tanning bed. Ordered it and had it delivered. I purchased new sheets with matching pillowcases for our bed. Put one of those continuous air fresheners in our bedroom. Set the little portable CD player on the dresser. Windexed the dresser mirror. Bought an old Luther Vandross CD. Took extra special care with my hygiene. Waited for my phone to ring.

It rang.

"Do you want to come and get this or do you want me to just send it back?"

"I don't understand," I said. My voice did that throaty crying thing again.

"Which word gives you a problem?" Amanda said.

"All of them," I said. "If you don't like that bed, pick out another one."

"You never asked me what I want."

"I'm asking now."

"Now's too late. Don't you get it, Kevin? Now's too late. I don't want to start crying again." Then she hung up.

***

The judge took my license. George loaned me the bicycle I'd helped him hang above the bar. That's all I'm saying about that.

***

I bought a big basket for the front of the bike.

I was allowed to keep my shift foreman's job at Dixie Cup. I live right in town. On rainy days, it was easy to catch a ride. The basket was like the one on the front of The Witch's bike, large enough to hold the groceries I need, strong enough to carry a case of beer or a Toto. Sometimes, I'd run up on one of The Bicycle Man's girls peddling some puss. Once, one coasted up beside me at a traffic light, right there on the courthouse square. She smiled but didn't attempt to conduct any business with me.

***

Sometimes truth comes too late.

***

There is a word for it. The word for it is lonely.

In case you're interested, the Animal Shelter is right past the Darlington County Detention Center, back off Highway 151. From the tiny cell window at the back of the jail, you can see the shelter. At night you can hear the lonely cries.

I wanted a dog.

The Animal Shelter guy said, "How are you going to get one home?" The name on his shirt said Delbert. We both looked at the red and white bike, at its basket. I'd taken the top sheet off our bed and folded it to make the basket soft. "I can't allow you to take a dog from here if you can't at least get him home."

"I'll drive safely," I said. My words had no more power with Delbert than they had had with Kurt, the trooper who put the cuffs on me. "I promise."

"A dog that don't know you ain't going to stay in that basket."

"I'll pet him with one hand and steer with the other," I said.

"No way."

"Give me a sick one." I said, "One that don't have any fight left in him. I'll get him home."

"Can't do it."

I looked at the cages. There were two or three dogs small enough to fit in my bicycle basket. None had much life left in him. I looked again at

Delbert. His hands were stuffed in the pockets of his khakis and he was making circles in the sand with his tennis shoe.

"Where do you live?" he said, not looking up at me. I told him. "Help me put your bicycle in the back of my truck." He pointed. "Then choose you a dog."

"Give me the sickest one," I said. "One that's half blind."

***

There are many kinds of love.

Some outrank others. He answers to "Boy." And like Jesus, he loved me before I loved him. He's very old, so old that his whiskers look like they're covered in thin ice. His black coat is sprinkled with gray. He sleeps a lot. Sometimes he dreams. And when he wakes, he stretches long and slow before he makes any attempt to move. He waddles. His rear end swings widely and his paws slap the floor like flippers. He is a dog of many breeds, the great, great grandfather to many.

What I learned was that when she left me, she didn't take this part of her and that part of her. She took something more than all her parts. Thoughts of sex with her were often on my mind, but I didn't think of her as sex. I never thought of her as parts anymore. What I'd lost was something I don't have words for.

Most nights, I put Boy in the basket and take him with me to The Paradise Lounge. George lets me park the bike inside. The working girls covet that bike. Boy sleeps in the basket while I laugh and drink and sing and tell stories.

There's a running bet on how long Boy will live, but it's pretty apparent that he's been adopted by everybody at The Paradise. I don't think about when he'll die. It's not something I like to imagine. But when he does, I'll have a silent service for him before I put him in the freezer. And after a time, some night when it seems the right thing to do, I'll take him out and prepare him for burial. I'll situate him comfortably in the basket of my bike and ride without haste. I'll peddle slowly, and think about things. I'll hum that old Ray Charles song with the words, I've made up my mind.

As we pick up speed down the long slope that leads past Amanda's house, I'll feel for balance, then lift my hands from the handlebars, extend my arms like wings. I'll take my feet from the pedals. As we pass her door, I'll tilt back my head and close my eyes. "I can't stop," I'll say to Boy. And then all the way down, until I get to the very bottom, until I have no more breath, I'll whisper her name.

Which Way You Going

I was watching this tall, skinny guy on the sidewalk at the corner of the McDonald's, about twenty feet away, while the girl working the drive-thru was fishing her brain out of the fry grease long enough to remember my order. If she hadn't been such a babe, I'd a smoked her. You know, waited till she slid open the little window, then hammered the Firebird, leaving enough black rubber in her nose to gag a cow. But she was a babe all right. And if there's two things I like, it's tits.

My eye kept drifting over to this skinny guy at the corner. He was about the skinniest dude I've ever seen, and tall too. I mean his bones looked like a bird's, and his face was covered with sweat as shiny and thick as lacquer. And check this out: He held a bag of ice that was melting. The plastic bag was filled with yellow light. He was just standing there like a statue or something with this plastic bag with a golden ball of light floating around in it like those two-headed babies you've seen in jars. I didn't know why, but I couldn't take my eyes off him. Maybe because he was such a ugly sonofabitch.

He hadn't looked in my direction, even when I goosed the Firebird's engine to remind the retard counter girl with the knockout body I was still waiting. He didn't turn and look at me once, not once. But goddamn it, it was like the guy had a flounder's eye buried in the side of his goddamn head or something. I mean it felt like he was looking.

Somebody said, "Your order, sir."

I turned down the volume real deliberate-like on my favorite Poison tape, you know, not looking up. But it wasn't the girl with the big knockers. It was the manager, a flesh tub with a fresh razor shave above his ears that looked like a pink slug stapled over each one. He was so fat he couldn't catch his breath. When he handed over my change, his shirt opened up and his fat, hairy fat showed. His nametag said Mac. I thought, what is this, some fucking joke? Big Mac, no can do.

I pumped the gas a couple of times, thinking Miss Tits might get the message, but she just stood staring into bimbo land, inking her scalp with a Bic pen. My plan was, I'd ask her if she wanted to party when she got off. I had it worked out. I'd say, "What time do you get off?" And she'd probably say, "'Bout eleven-thirty." Then I'd say, "Can I watch?" Then she'd finally get it and laugh and I'd ask her out for real. Instead, what I get is a cross between Ronald McDonald and the Pillsbury

Doughboy—and Mister Flounder eye with the mostly water bag hunkered like a goddamn refugee. I pressed in the clutch, shifted into first, and eased forward.

I hadn't got ten feet when I had to stop for a old Chrysler wagon full of daycare convicts to back its slow ass out and find the goddamn street. Then I saw that the tall, skinny guy was going to ask me for a ride.

"Which way you going?" he said.

"Which way you going?"

"Don't matter."

"No way," I said.

"Come on, Man."

"I don't trust your ass," I said.

"Cause I'm black, ain't it?"

"I don't trust nobody. How do you know I won't drive a few miles south, pull over, and splatter your brains out with a tire iron. Take your money."

"But I ain't got nothing but this," he looked down at the dripping plastic bag he was holding, "and it's melting."

"Yeah, but I'm going to a party. That ice would come in handy. I might X your ass for some party ice."

The guy disappeared back into the shade where he'd come from, back into whatever it was he'd been seeing, as if I hadn't even been there.

"Tough shit, Sherlock!" I yelled, pulling away.

If the guy heard me, I don't know it.

On the street, I went through the gears like love grease, feeling the G-force press my back into the seat, feeling good. It was then I figured I'd drive the hour and a half to Myrtle Beach, check out the babes. In July, it don't matter that it's a Wednesday. Every day's poon day at the beach in July. Besides, since I'd lost my dead-end, loser's, dip-shit job, every day was poon day. Party-time-is-anytime-and-any-time-is-party-time, so let's parrr-ty. That was rap. I hate that rap shit.

I figured I'd drive around for a while, till it got too fucking hot to ride, then go to The Showhouse maybe, where the babes put it in your face. I'd have to nurse the five-buck drinks, take those suckers easy, make 'em last, since I was a little low on cash. Besides I'd have to drive back, unless I got lucky. I figured I'd find a party somewhere. There are women everywhere at the beach. I'd get one with bad teeth and a nice ass and a room, one of those goo-goo-eyed babes from Michigan or somewhere who wants to get laid at the beach, you know, like on MTV. I figured if they got a pulse and a room key we got two things in common, you know what I mean?

I'd have to remember to call my mom, though. I keep reminding her I'm 21 now, but if I don't check in, she'll be the first to call the parole officer on my ass, blow the whistle on me, the bitch. Really, I love her. She worries a lot. I haven't been what you might call a Beaver Cleaver of a son. To tell you the truth, she's about the best woman in the world. I'd do anything for her, you know, if I could. Anyway, I was on Highway 501, resting on 70 miles an hour when I remembered my new sunglasses, the ones with the orange and black frames. I checked them out in the mirror. Killer. Then I took the first bite of my Quarter Pounder.

***

I about shit when the cops started pounding on the goddamn door. I was so fucking out of it that I couldn't remember my name. All I knew was that it was dark, I'm freezing, and I don't know where I am. And I can't feel my legs. Then I hear what sounds like a sledge hammer on the metal door. I hear voices; then the door opens and all I can think is my parole officer is gonna nail my ass. Somebody hits the lights and somebody else pulls the drapes. I'm lying in a tub of ice, staring like a deer in the headlights, about to shit. It takes me a second to realize they're not all cops. I look around and this tall, skinny guy has a needle in my arm. Then I'm moving like a motherfucker and I can hear the siren and I'm thinking, far out. Fucking far out.

I don't remember much shit from the next day or two. I mean I can tell you a lot of shit but I can't put it in any order, and some of it may not be true. I mean I kept trying to explain to my mom that I had been outside a crowded train station when some loony bastard opened up with an Uzi or something, mowing people down. The whole crowd went bananas. The guy just ran around shooting, I told her. And I couldn't find the station and I didn't have a ticket and there was no fucking body to help. It was a day or two before she could convince me that all that train station stuff was a dream. They had these tubes and shit in me, even in my dick, and I slept a lot.

There were two cops there when I finally woke up enough to talk with the doctor. One of the cops couldn't have been much older than me, and you could just tell he didn't know shit. The other one did most of the talking. He was like the dad of the two. He gave me this papa-daddy smile, showing a gap between his teeth that probably made him spit champion of Cornhole County or something. "How you feeling, son?" he said, like it made a shit to him.

I looked from him to my mom who had this big I-been-suffering-all-my-life look on her face. Then I saw the doctor, who looked like cigarettes and coffee and no sleep in weeks.

"Like shit," I said. "Feel like living shit."

"How did this happen?" Papa-daddy said in this sort of funeral home voice.

I looked from him to the doctor, then back at him.

"Tell us everything you can. Don't leave anything out."

"What do you mean?" I said.

"Begin from the time you arrived at The Showhouse. Your car was left there."

I'd even forgotten I'd driven to the beach at all. Let alone gone to the tit capital of the South.

"Yeah, I went there."

"Who did you meet there? Tell us everything you can."

I had to think. Then I was back at the train station and I couldn't find my goddamn ticket and they were taking people away in body bags, black ones. Then I remembered that I had been in the bar. Then I remembered the rest, to a point. I didn't want to tell it all. Not with my mom there and all. Everybody was looking at me, waiting. The old cop had been to principal school or something cause he knew just to sit there like a goddamn toad and let me stew until I finally said something.

"I went in to cool off, you know. It was hotter'n a muther." I knew not to look at my mom, but the old fart-face cop wasn't making it easy on me. He still didn't say anything. "I had a beer and watched the show."

"Who did you meet there?"

"Some woman."

"What was her name?"

"I don't remember."

"Tell us what you do remember. Take your time. We're in no hurry. Don't leave anything out." He crossed his arms and leaned back in his chair.

"I'm sitting at one of those little tables off to the side," I say. "I'd almost finished my first beer. It was between songs and this woman sits down beside me."

"What did she look like, can you describe her?"

"Killer. She was in this white halter." For a second I saw her sitting there. "She asked me to buy her a drink, and I'm thinking she looks too good for a hooker. I mean she looked like a cheerleader or something."

Now the Eagle Scout cop, the young prick with the double starched haircut, spoke. "Did she, ah, proposition you?" We all looked at him for a second like he was the stupidest bag of shit you ever saw.

"What did she say?" the older guy asked, breaking the ice finally.

"Exactly, you mean?"

"As best you can recall."

"She said, 'That beer looks sooo cold. Look,' she said, 'it still has little slivers of ice in it.' She smiled in that buy-me-a-beer look."

The old fart chuckled, giving me that snake grin. "I know that look," he said. Now he was being confidential, the cocksucker.

"So I say to her, 'I'm kinda low on cash.' She runs her hand real slow up my jeans to my pocket." I remembered my bleeding heart mother is right there, but it's too late. "She gives my pocket a little squeeze and says, 'That's too bad. Let me buy,' she says. So I say fuckin' A." I look from one cop to the other because even I can't believe this babe was buying me drinks. But that part is true, swear to God. They don't even bat an eye.

"How many beers did she buy?"

"Two or three more."

"Where did she tell you she was taking you?"

I looked at my mom like, don't you want to take a hike, you old bitch? Or do you want another quart of thirty-weight I've-been-a-failed-mother? She just sits there like a fucking nun or something. So I think, fuck you. Fasten your seatbelt, you old cunt.

"Said she was taking me to her hotel."

"Which one?"

"The Radisson."

"Did you go there?"

"I don't remember."

"What is the last thing you do remember?"

"I don't remember."

"Try."

I was getting just a little tired of this cat and mouse bullshit.

"What was she driving?"

"A Hummer—silver, fancy motherfucker."

"Tell us about the man," says the Mr. GQ cop.

"If you know all this shit, why you asking me?"

"Did you notice if the tags were out of state?" says the one in charge.

"No."

"Was he in the SUV?"

"Ask me something you don't already know, why don't you."

"He was driving, right?"

"Let me make this easy for you, dude. The chick says she wants to screw my eyeballs out. You follow me? I say let's get down. You hear what I'm saying? She asks if I've got a kinky mind. I say my head's got more kinks than Buckwheat's. She says what you into, looking down, like at my whammy bar."

"I think I'll go outside for a smoke," says mom, digging down in the blue jean pocketbook she's been carrying since her hippie days. Bitch has a tattoo on her droopy ass. She takes out her lighter and some Kleenex. We all watch her leave. The old doctor, who hasn't said a fucking word, gives me a look like I'm keeping him from a very important conversation with his stockbroker. We all watch the door close behind the Mother of God. Then the old man kind of bears down on me.

"So she's giving the old meat man here this porno look," I say. "She says, 'Would you care if someone watches?' 'Who?' I say. 'Would you?' she says, giving the old pork a little pull. I just look at her. 'My husband,' she says. 'I ain't into any queer shit,' I say."

"What happened in the SUV," says Loverboy cop. "Did you get a good look at the man, the driver?"

The fucker.

"So, I say to her, 'Baby, I got the face if you got the place.'"

"How long were you in the Hummer?" says Sonnyboy.

"You tell me, okay?" I'm pissed now. "You know all the shit. Why the fuck you even talking to me, dude? I'm the guy with a fucking hole in his back. You're the fucker whose 'spose to be telling me shit; so I'll fucking shut up and let you tell the story, okay? Let's hear it, Mr. Unfucking-solved Mysteries."

He just gives me this superior I'm-here-to-protect-and-serve look.

"Ain't it time for lunch or medicine or something?" I say to the doc.

"We're almost done," says Captain Kirk with the fangs. "Go ahead."

Now I make these fuckers squirm for a few seconds.

"So you see, I think we're gonna do it right there in the van. I'm thinking her and her queer-bait husband spend their vacations having guys bang the bitch while her husband spanks his monkey in the driver's seat, or some shit. So I like go for the bitch, you know, for her tits. But she says, 'Let's have a drink on the way to the hotel.' She opens the refrigerator and takes out vodka, Absolut, that expensive shit, and some tonic. That's all I remember."

"So you really didn't get much of a look at the man then," says the old geezer. He and Mr. Junior Suntan King exchange a look that says they already know the answer.

"Man," I say, "if you'd seen those tits." Nobody said anything. "That's it," I said, looking around at everybody. "That's it."

We all just sat there like everybody was waiting for somebody to say the blessing. "Wellll?" I say. Nobody says anything. I look from one to the other. "Wellll?" I say again. "Why did the sonofabitch stab me in the fucking back?"

And now Doctor Spock, or whatever the fuck his name is, who's been sitting there like he was taking a constipated shit for the past fifteen minutes, pipes up. "You weren't stabbed," he says. "Somebody drugged you and removed one of your kidneys."

I just look at him. I think I'm going to bust out laughing. "What the fuck? My fucking kidney? You're shittin' me," I say.

"There is a black market value in organs."

"Whoa," I say. "You mean somebody operated on me? Actually stole one of my goddamn kidneys? You got to be shittin'. You fuckers are jerking me around, aren't you? Some motherfucker stole my fucking kidney?" I looked all around. "You assholes better be talking to me. You better be telling me some shit. I want to know who cut me, you shitheads. I want to hear some shit from all you motherfuckers."

They just sat there like three hear-no, see-no, speak-no, motherfucking monkeys. The fuckers.

***

It was near Halloween when the doctor quit writing prescriptions for my Demerol. I've got this heavy psycho shit going through my head, I told him, shit I don't even like to think about. I still hurt, I said. He just tilts his head so that he looks at me over his little rectangle queer glasses and hands back the empty plastic bottle the pills come in. I try the old pharmacist at CVS, but he ain't fooled. I drop the empty plastic bottle in a trick-or-treat bag on the way out.

There's this shit I can't stop thinking about. I figure it's time for a little of the old me to come back.

So I'm sitting in one of those wooden seats that must have come from an old movie theater. You know, the hard as hell seats that fold up. Tripping my brains out. Tripping my fucking brains out. My plan was this: To drop the acid, dump the old lady at the bus station, fart around for a while, then get to the club as soon as the doors open for the Poison reunion show. Way I figured it, I'd be peaking big-time about the last thirty minutes of the show, when the fireworks went off.

What I didn't figure—kick my own ass for this shit—what I didn't figure was my retard mother. The whore goes to church camp somewhere near Asheville every October. She always wants me to drive her up, but I know she just thinks she can trap me in the car for half a day and give me the God Squad treatment. She thinks I'll get there and suddenly hear the Word of The Savior. You can catch a bus, I tell her.

But then I've got to deliver her ass to the station, which I do after I drop, and guess what? The bitch has the fucking time wrong, missed the goddamn bus. So now I got to wait the hour and twenty minutes with her for the next bus. I sit there rushing like a motherfucker, watching the walls bend at the corners, and hearing every fucking thing. Somewhere in the station somebody says, "kidney stoned." Swear to God. Then I'm laughing like a lunatic. It's like the funniest shit I ever heard. My stupid as shit mom, who's sitting there like a Hallmark card somebody pissed on, thinks I'm laughing cause I'm so mad about having to sit there for the motherfucking bus to hell. So she doesn't say anything to me, which is good, cause I'm getting off like a bastard, and I can't talk for shit. Everything's that damned funny.

I'm sitting with my back to the sun, which is getting low now. Pretty soon the light begins to change to that yellow that you get in October. I'm digging the shit out of it, watching the color of everything turn golden. I mean it was like being inside something that was alive, and you were in it and it was changing all around you. It was like you were floating around inside something, and there was all this soft yellow light. I was out there. I was going off. Then mother stepped in front of me, with that light all over her, and suddenly the light was coming from inside her. "I wish you'd come with me," she said.

By this time I couldn't move. I was like all balled up inside. I just looked at her with pupils like moons, I just fucking know. Her eyes got all watery for a second. Then she walked out of the station and got on the bus. She sat beside the window like a bright light, profiled in the shadow. When the bus pulled away, the whole fucking earth shook, swear to God.

I tried to get my shit together, but I knew the only way I was going to get my ass out of there was to plan ahead, to plan my moves and to talk myself to my car. But every time I got about halfway through the plan I'd be thinking about something else. I did get this far: I'd wait until the next bus arrived. Then when the people were unloading and boarding, I'd just slide my ass out, undetected. I waited.

Across the way was this old concentration camp-looking fucker. Must have been seven feet tall, all sprawled out from one of those little wooden chairs. And the motherfucker is shaking like he's freezing or something. I don't want to look at him. He's giving me the damned creeps. But it's like him and me are the only fuckers in the bus station, and I can't move and this vibrating corpse can't stop shaking. He ain't going anywhere and I ain't going anywhere. It's just him and me. The sun is going down and the light is washing over this old guy and it's getting to be red light that covers him and he's shaking like one freezing motherfucker, and it's like no matter where I look he's there.

I try closing my eyes. At first, it's like I'm being squeezed from all sides. Then, whoaaa, it's like the shit went into high gear and I'm tripping so hard I'm about to zoom from the old body. Then everything begins to shake: the floor, the seat, me, the shit on the walls.

After fucking forever, I remember I can open my eyes. Everything is shaking and this old bastard is doing like five thousand RPMs and the whole place is red. The light is red. Then there is this wild wave of voices.

People are pouring through the door. I hear a bus engine. Then the driver shuts off the diesel, and everything but the old man stops shaking. I want to spring out of my seat and run like a motherfucker, but my heart is racing like hell. The fucker hurts, it's running so hard. I can't catch my breath. I can't breathe for shit. Then I see this woman coming toward me. And I know she is going to sit beside me. Like fucking will or something. She's about two years pregnant, and sure as hell she sits one seat over. And now I'm looking at this huge pregnant woman, at her stomach, you know. I know I must have made her feel like a freak or something, but this acid was kicking my ass.

For a time I tried to remember where my car was. I had no fucking idea. Couldn't even remember which door I'd come in.

Another bus unloaded, and now the place was getting crowded and there were these crying babies and black bitches yelling at them and shit, and I was beginning to get a little paranoid. There were people like moving all around me, kind of circling me. And I'm thinking, I got to get the fuck out of here.

Then this fat guy with thick glasses and sideburns starts talking to himself. He's carrying a gym bag, one of those brown half-moon-looking jobs they don't make anymore. He sets it down, then he picks it up. Then he sets it down and starts to unzip it. Then picks it up again, talking to himself the whole time. Talking this spooky mumbo jumbo. Then I hear the fucker say something about killing somebody, or that's what I think he says. Then I know he's packing in that bag and the fucker's going to open up on everybody. He's gonna walk as casual as a mailman through the station mowing people down. There's going to be blood and shit and bodies everywhere. I look around for help.

The pregnant woman has her eyes shut, her arms folded over her crotch, which pulls her thin dress over her about-to-explode belly. Then I look back at the guy with the gym bag, who's still mumbling, but now he really is unzipping the fucker. It's like I'm the only one who knows, and I'm seeing my path to tackle the bastard. I'm visualizing. I glance to make sure the coast is clear before I nail his ass. Then this happened: It moved. The woman's whole stomach moved. I saw it through her dress. This thing inside her moved. I could see its outline. Blew my fucking mind. You could see it. Goddamn, I thought, there's something alive inside her and it's moving. She's got something alive in there. There's something alive in there trying to fucking get born.

A bolt of lightning knocked the ever-living fuck out of me. Light everywhere. Something was going to happen and I couldn't do a thing about it. This shit was coming down, all this shit, and I couldn't stop it. There was no stopping it.

Then I was crying like a baby. I don't even like to think about it.

This old shaky voice says, "Are you all right, son?" I was crying so hard I couldn't look up. And then the pregnant woman whispers, "Jesus."

I was standing outside between two parked buses. The fuckers must have been seven miles long.

I was outside. I was alone outside. I just walked to the first place where I could get out of sight. It was dark as hell.

Then I walked for a little while longer. I didn't know where in hell I was. I really didn't. I don't like to think about it. And I was afraid to walk and afraid to stop walking. I sat on the curb in some neighborhood and boo-hooed like a fucking baby for I don't know how long. Sometimes, you know, I can't stop thinking about this shit. I had to get the hell out of there. I wanted to walk and keep on walking until I knew where I was. I even ran as far as I could. As I was catching my breath, I could hear my heart beating in my ears. Then I heard one of the buses start up. I wouldn't go so far that I couldn't hear the buses, I thought. Then I was someplace else, sitting on the curb, not knowing where the fuck I was but not crying anymore. I was just sitting in the middle of the darkness of no fucking place. I don't even like to think about it. Hoping somebody would see me and take me home.

You know, just waiting.

Twelve Tips for Writing an Unpublishable Story

Tip One: Avoid short, catchy titles.

***

Tip Two: Introduce characters that your readers will soon forget.
 FRANK, OWNER OF CITY IN THE SKY BINGO PARLOR
 The owner of the City In The Sky bingo parlor, a thick-necked guy from New Jersey named Frank, exaggerated his Gambino-esque accent and dyed his hair black as a crow's wing to show that he was a tough guy. But on Saturday nights, he sported a blonde wig and red high heels, and lip-synced Barbara Streisand songs at Whispers, the gay club he owned off Highway 501 on the way to Myrtle Beach. Frank, a Lebanese who claimed to be Italian, had mastered makeup and jewelry; through their careful use, he could seemingly shrink his neck the way a lizard can. Frank, the Lebanese bingo parlor-owning, cross-dressing Streisand look-alike, closed every show with a tear-jerking rendition of A Star Is Born.

***

Tip Three: Mock Christians of convenience.
 THE MOTHER OF DORIS RICH
 Forty-two years old and socially religious, Doris Rich's mother loved the Bible, though she'd never read it. Instead, she devoured trashy Romance novels, which served as her intellectual and moral compass and explained why events in TV soap operas (which she called The Stories) really did make sense. And she adored gin. You might say that Mrs. Rich loved Jesus and sin and gin. Blind to the conflicts inherent in her trinity, Mrs. Rich lived comfortably in that space where the Bible, the soaps and the gin overlapped. "I am what I am," she would proclaim when her passions collided.
 On those nights when Mrs. Rich's id boiled, when she felt so trashy good that no manual dexterity or battery-powered technology could sate her, she'd drive to the Paradise Lounge in Darlington, where she'd drink Cosmopolitans with extra sugar on the rim and talk to the first man in her league about how in August it was too hot to wear panties.
 "I am what I am," she'd purr.
 Then she would scoot her hand up the man's thigh in a little roller coaster act, and say, "This is the way God made me." She'd give his

meaty flesh a squeeze, sending his testicles scurrying like hermit crabs, and coo, "God don't make no junk." And the man would smile proudly as his glands engorged and think, But lucky for me he sure do make some trash.

You might say that Mrs. Rich considered herself a scholar in the academy of common sense, hard knocks, and country wisdom; a modern woman, having suffered the burdens of single parenthood buffered only by the house at the country club that Mr. Rich was paying for, his flush 401-K, and half his retirement if only the son-of-a-bitch would retire; and the proud proprietress of sexual prerogatives vested in God's work and trumpeted in every worthwhile woman's magazine.

You might say that Mrs. Rich was an ignorant white-trash slut.

***

Tip Four: Offend readers from across the social and political spectrum, especially editor types.

DORIS RICH

Unable to read or write, Mrs. Rich's daughter Doris, who possessed only one leg, sailed through college, majoring in Sociology and minoring in Gender Studies. Her professors gave her perfect scores, for in the Forrest Gump worldview so favored by those disciplines she had already earned her marks; she was the most "Other" in each of her classes: ignorant, sincere, and one-legged. When her professors glanced up from their lectures on hierarchy, victimization, and oppression, Doris would shout, "Bingo!" and heads would nod a mass amen.

At graduation, the commencement speaker—Doris's academic advisor, Dr. DeMint—choked up when quoting a pilfered passage from Doris's thesis, entitled "Less Is More: A Testimonial to Perseverance in the Face of Persecution." (Its original title, plagiarized from a Tillie Olson short story, had been "I Stand Here On One Leg Ironing." But after a writing center tutor asked, "Where is 'here,' and whose leg are you standing on?" the two brainstormed the revision). At the conclusion of her speech, Dr. DeMint looked up with bubbled tears on her pitted, chubby cheeks and waited stoically until everybody in the auditorium stood en masse.

Everybody but Doris, who didn't much feel like it. "Bingo!" she shouted instead.

Exerting every ounce of her hierarchical power over the silent audience, Dr. DeMint eventually allowed the twitching crowd to sit. Then with a blank, deaf-mute I'm-watching-TV gaze, she waited a full-term pregnant pause before drawing a breath that would rival a blowfish and whispered into the microphone that Doris was graduating cum laude. The crowd, in a single ejaculatory gesture, leapt in delirium. "Cum laude!" the professor shouted again, her microphone squealing like a squashed cat.

"Bingo!" Doris echoed.

Over the applause, her mother staggered to her feet. Grinning like a chimp and slapping her hands like a penguin in a meth lab, she announced to the man beside her: "She gets that from me. I'm multi-orgasmic, you know. And loud? Whew!" she shouted with a dismissive flutter of her hand.

***

Tip Five: Offend the "challenged."
DORIS AND MRS. RICH'S HOMELIFE, PART 1

God had given Doris all of Mrs. Rich's id but only one of her legs. In the first order, Doris blamed Mr. Rich for the birth defect. It was just too easy not to. Second, she blamed in equal parts her mother and the gin. Next she blamed God, but got little satisfaction, for from a very early age her mother had wagged her finger and slurred, "It is what it is," and "I am what I am," before diving into her hymnal adaptation of a KC and the Sunshine Band disco number. "That's the way uh-huh, uh-huh, God planned it," she sang, taking Doris's tiny hands in her own and dancing around her as if she were a Maypole. Now, when Doris had silent conversations with Mr. Big, she skipped the obvious question for something like, "Why couldn't you have just made it my left leg? I look like the mailman when I drive the car."

Doris's deeply internalized id produced a rabid surliness in her. You might say she was one pissed off one-legged woman. Sometimes when Mrs. Rich ricocheted around the house to get Doris dressed in time for church, she screamed, "Where are your damned shoes?" And something about Mrs. Rich's use of the plural form brought out the worst in Doris, something that after graduating cum laude in Sociology and Gender Studies made her exclaim, "I'd believe in God if he'd only made me an albino African-American one-legged lesbian!"

"Be happy with what you've got!" Ms. Rich bellowed back before scurrying for the bottle of Bombay Sapphire hidden in the laundry basket.

Doris and Mrs. Rich found parity and common ground in their ignorance. Despite her mastery of Sociology and Gender Studies, Doris's expertise was in theater: her education had immersed her in stage methods for dramatically expressing shallow emotions and small ideas. She learned to reduce popular notions from Critical Theory to a set of words and phrases as universal and interchangeable as a set of ratchet wrenches. She had simply gone to Infoshop News, copied a vocabulary list she couldn't read, placed each word or phrase on a separate slip of paper, and stored the slips in a coffee can where she kept her weed. To write a paper, she'd roll a joint, pull out the slips at random, and type what she saw.

The original version of "I Stand Here On One Leg Ironing" began like this: "Post-anarchists valorize binary structures that are crimethink-esque, multicultural, and in the now. The Situationists' layers of rhetoric critically assert that the opposite don't make it so by rolling together semi-related tendencies into a pastiche/collage, not a definitive narrative trajectory of essentialist, anti-colonial readings but of mystical dialects, a blanket dismissal of a highly variegated history."

You might think that this vocabularied artillery gave her tactical advantage in the exchange of mother/daughter abuses. But when Doris machine-gunned her mother with a battery of postmodern verbiage, Mrs. Rich just tilted her cherry red nose high and said, "Bullshit."

***

Tip Six: Avoid plot development; fill your pages with back story.
   YOUNG DORIS GOES TO SCHOOL
   You might say that intellectually speaking Doris and her mother were head-to-head midgets, literally cut from the same cloth. After all, Doris had been home-schooled by Mrs. Rich, a neo-con Christian who believed in family values (which she called "family falues)."

"No Christian who believes in family falues would submit her one-legged daughter to the immoral cruelties of public school. I can teach that myself," Mrs. Rich explained to her bobble head, gin drinking, neo-con Christian friends. Also, from deep inside her id, Mrs. Rich was a closet racist who hated dark-skinned bipeds. So she felt fully qualified to teach Doris and to keep it simple: "That's the way, uh-huh, uh-huh, God wants it," she sang.

In late August when the other kids were in the classroom, young Doris tucked a Penney's catalog under one arm and pogoed out to the backyard pool where Mrs. Rich sipped gin and sunbathed sans top. She dropped the catalog beside her mom and said, "Let's begin my lessons."

"Not today." Mrs. Rich lifted the cotton balls off her nipples to examine her tan.

When autumn arrived, Mrs. Rich took out the Bingo game. "Time for school!"

"What are we studying today!?" young Doris shouted, leaping and slamming her hands together. "A-B-C's? Numbers? Words?"

"Yes."

"What first?" Doris sang out.

"All three. Doris, stop that! You're making me seasick."

"At once!" the young girl exclaimed. "Oh boy oh boy ohboy ohboy!!"

At which point Mrs. Rich administered the game of Bingo, which accounted for the sum of Doris's education and the only happy moments she and her mother shared.

***

Tip Seven: Bore your reader.

A NEW DORIS EMERGES

Doris's college education was exactly what her id had ordered. An education consists of a body of knowledge, a set of skills, and an array of abilities. But these alone do not distinguish the cum laudes from the rest. A particular disposition toward learning is what adds the shine. And that disposition, that attitude, Doris intuited, was what you might call "pissed off." In the dim halls of learning, she was introduced to a world beyond bingo. Here she acquired a bold and abrasive terrier-like social manner. Doris Rich soon mastered the nuances of pissed-offedness and became the envy of fellow students and the prize of her professors. Her classmates, whose faces included every hue in a watercolor starter set, were mostly women, though her professors recruited some gender bending males.

The classroom was lively in an evangelical way that made Doris feel right at home. When things got dull, the professor would open her bag of Southern white male anecdotes, and the class would go as wild as piranhas at a chicken gizzard-eating contest. Even the most docile student would wail and sob and flail about like a Pentecostal biped in a meth lab. But outside the classroom most reverted to their shadow lives. Not Doris. Her id ignited in passion, and she obeyed its command.

After a particularly inspiring class, she sometimes entered the Student Union on her crutches, jutting her carriage forward like a buzzard on a precipice, and set her sights on an unsuspecting cheerleader type. When her mark looked up in astonishment and fear, Doris lifted her skirt above her nub and shouted: "Tooouch it! Feeeel it!"

The coed would shrink back and search the room for air support. "No! No! Get away from me!" she'd plead as Doris humped her hips into the co-ed's horror-stricken face.

"Feel my pain!" Doris shouted. "No Pain, No Gain! I am the OTHER!" And the white girl would boo-hoo as Doris glared and glowered over her as if the young Presbyterian were chopped steak.

Another time, right outside her advisor's office, she turned on the college's star quarterback. "Is it true that black men are repulsed by the idea of giving oral pleasure to their female lovers?" she barked. Leaning in, Doris dropped her head back a notch, vulture-like, and gave him the wandering fish eye.

"I ain't going down on no one-legged white girl, if that's what you mean."

Doris's head began to bob and weave, and her hand flopped like a flounder out of water. Her fingers formed odd shapes like a talking deaf person's. "You can't do the grine till you've had some O' dis behine," she said, giving her rump a solid whop. Then: "You ain't had no grub till you had some O' dis nub," she said, throwing the one leg up can-can fashion, bringing it to rest on his broad shoulder, then doing what she called "the magic bellows act" in his face.

You might say that Doris gained a reputation.

***

Tip Eight: Introduce the central conflict somewhere in the middle.
THE GAME, NOT THE DOG

"You drive," Mrs. Rich said as she and Doris made for the Honda.

"No way."

"The judge said I'm out of second chances," Mrs. Rich said. "What would folks think if you let your mama get another D.U.I.?" Then: "WWJD?" she asked, bearing down on her daughter.

They stood at the rear of the car. "But we look like lesbians on a date when I drive," Doris whined.

"That's the way, uh-huh, uh-huh, God planned it," Mrs. Rich said, opening the passenger door.

Doris refused to speak on the drive to the City In The Sky bingo parlor. Nor did she follow Mrs. Rich's suggestions for safe driving. When she drew stares from two Lynyrd Skynyrd fans at a busy intersection, Doris threw her arm around Mrs. Rich's shoulder and shouted over Free Bird, "Take a picture, you fags. It'll last longer." Then she drew her eyebrows way up and made her eyes wide like a Chihuahua's, flicked her tongue at them like a viper, and pinched Mrs. Rich's right nipple.

"You pervert!" yelped her mother.

The Skynyrd boys pumped their middle finger at Doris.

When they pulled into the City In The Sky parking lot, Mrs. Rich rubbed circles on her breast with her palm. "That hurt."

"Shut up and get my crutches."

***

Tip Nine: Tell, don't show.
BINGO!
Police officers threatened to handcuff Doris Rich. She'd overturned a dozen tables, and two EMS teams administered oxygen to terrorized bingo-playing geriatrics.

"Stand back!" Doris cried, wielding a crutch. The cops stopped.

"You have to come with us," one officer said.

Doris's face purpled up as she raised her crutches like goal posts. Her eyes rolled back like a shark's, and when her face was the color of an eggplant she shuddered and shouted, "Fuuuuuuuuuck you," descending to a harmonic frequency that only Darth Vader could rival.

When the cop reached for his pepper spray, Doris began speaking in tongues, babbling word for word passages from Foucault, Derrida, Fish, and Said. Meanwhile, Mrs. Rich, trapped like a terrorist hostage between her crazed daughter and a concrete wall, shouted, "Poltergeist! Poltergeist!" then began to spin slowly on her axis, eyes shut tight, hands covering her ears, chanting "George W., George W., George W."

The police report said that during a high stakes bingo game, Doris claimed that she had won a $5,000 prize and repeatedly hollered "Bingo!" when the winning number was announced. But the caller didn't hear her. She couldn't stand because she had only one leg. The caller, a white male, produced another number, which resulted in winning cards for two other white male players.

Attached to the typed police report was a post-it note in the officer's hand. He often made separate notes for himself when he anticipated being called to testify. He had written, "Ms. Doris Rich was one pissed off one-legged woman."

***

Tip Ten: Circle back to a character that your readers have forgotten.
I'M FRANK. REMEMBER ME?
Frank was searching his dresser for mascara when the phone rang.

"We got a bone to pick," Doris Rich said.

"Who is this? Who gave you this number?"

"Never you nevermind. I want my muuneee," she said in her best Sling Blade voice.

"Talk to my attorney."

"I ain't dealing with that pencil dick twerp no more. I'm dealing direct."

"Who gave you this number?" He heard a click on the other end.

Doris had obtained the number from her once upon a time advisor, Dr. DeMint. The woman had read a newspaper account of the City In The Sky mayhem and immediately fired off a 2,000-word op-ed piece arguing that the Florence Morning News had no right to bring its vested power against a one-legged cum laude, and that most of what was wrong with Western culture oozed like pus from every paragraph of the newspaper's story.

The two women had met at Starbuck's where Doris learned that Frank was gay.

***

Tip Eleven: Ignore plausibility.
WHISPERS

Wearing only bra and panties, Doris stood on one leg in front of her open closet mindlessly scratching her nub the way another might scratch her chin. "Butch or babe," she whispered to herself. Doris had never been to a gay club. Her mother, who thought they were attending the Florence Little Theater, wore her square dancing dress because, like a stovepipe, it covered the wrinkles in her neck. And it made torpedoes of her breasts. Mrs. Rich was stylin' in front of Doris's full-length mirror while Doris pondered her fashion choices.

"I'll drive," Doris offered; she had invited Mrs. Rich along for cover. "You go ahead and make yourself another gin drink, Mama."

"I reckon I will," Mrs. Rich said to the mirror. "It's a long time between acts."

Mrs. Rich finished her toddy on the drive to the gay bar she thought was the Little Theater and then reached for the car radio. Doris ignored as best she could her mother's channel selection. The Wobblers were singing, If You Ain't Here After What I'm Here After, You'll Be Here After I'm Gone. Doris kept her eyes on the road as Mrs. Rich laid her right hand atop her left, patting one knee and then the other in four-four time. Doris drew a deep breath and bit her lip when Mrs. Rich's head began flopping metronomically from side to side.

But when Mrs. Rich began singing, Doris, without inflection, ordered her to "Shut the fuck up."

Still patty-caking and bobbing, her mother replied, just as unemphatically, "That wasn't very Christian-like."

***

Tip Twelve: Convenience, sentimentality, and the rabbit in the hat are your friends.

WHISPERS II

As Doris and Mrs. Rich stepped inside Whispers, Doris's pupils spiraled open and the scene came into focus. The club's interior was dark, and red candlelight flickered over the dozens of cheap red tablecloths. Barry Manilow oozed from the jukebox. The booths and tables were taken, but there were seats to the left, at the bar. A cluster of couples danced at the far end of the room in front of the riser that served as a stage.

"Remodeled," Mrs. Rich noted. "When I saw Fiddler on the Roof here last year they didn't have a dance floor." A Gloria Gaynor song began. Mrs. Rich raised her arms and tap-danced a little Gypsy hoedown.

Someone called Doris's name; the silhouette of an arm waved near the stage. It was her college advisor, Professor DeMint.

"C'mon," Doris said to her mother.

When she started across the room, a wide, smiling path opened for Doris, and faces she'd never seen said, "Evenin'" and "Howdy." Mrs. Rich followed in her wake, eyes half-closed, arms high and pumping like pistons to the music, hips way out in front of the rest of her like she was dancing the limbo. By the time they reached the table, Dr. DeMint had pulled out their chairs. Dressed like a safari leader, the professor wore hiking boots, khaki shorts and shirt, and a turtle shell hat. She and Doris exchanged a comrade's embrace. DeMint offered her hand to Mrs. Rich.

"I recognize you," Mrs. Rich said. "At...at—"

"Commencement?" Dr. DeMint suggested.

"You wore that pretty black smock. But I didn't care much for the hat."

"Let's have a drink," the professor said, taking Doris's crutches.

"I'll second that emotion," chimed Mrs. Rich, looking about the dark room. Dr. DeMint and Doris huddled in fierce conversation, their gibberish accentuated by DeMint's punching the tablecloth with her pointer finger.

"There are times when our moral obligations collide," she said, tossing back the remains of her second bourbon. "But I must remind you that in this case—one in which the scars of gender Otherness are weighed against the prejudice of physically challenged Otherness—we need only look to the principle of justice to see the light."

Doris tilted her head like a quadruped studying abstract art.

"Aside from his sexual preference," DeMint continued, "Frank is a man." Slowly raising her glass, the professor gave Doris a penetrating eyeball-to-eyeball. "Tear his friggin' heart out," she whispered.

"Bingo," said Doris.

After drinks were served all around, Mrs. Rich watched their server walk away. There was something in that walk.

"Damn," Mrs. Rich said, tugging at Professor DeMint's arm, "He's pretty. What's his name?"

DeMint gave her a look reserved for the severely challenged and patted Mrs. Rich's wrist. "It's Shawn," she said.

"Prettiest skin I ever saw on a man," Mrs. Rich replied. "He ought to be on The Stories."

DeMint gave that scornful, superior look to Doris, who mirrored it back as she had been taught to do.

"Bingo," Doris said.

"There—. " Professor DeMint said with a gesture, looking over Doris's shoulder.

A song that had been popular when Mrs. Rich was a child filled the room, and she turned to see two pillars of light on the stage. Into the first stepped their server, Shawn.

"That's Sonny!" Mrs. Rich exclaimed as Shawn sang the opening lines to I Got You Babe.

Frank stepped into the second column of light.

"That's him?" Doris whispered.

As Frank/Cher sang, the crowd swooned with every line. Doris felt Frank Cher's eyes on her. When Frank Cher's arm reached outside that light, it reached for Doris. His tears at the end of the song, the tears over the "I got you babe, I got you babe," almost made her forget about the scissors in her purse and about her bloody intent.

"I didn't know Cher was a Negro," Mrs. Rich shouted over the music. "Ouch! Somebody stepped on my foot."

The lights faded with the song, and when the stage was dark, the crowd roared to its feet—except for Doris, who experienced a mysterious pang of intense inner conflict.

Mrs. Rich's id coiled up like a jack-in-the-box as she watched Sonny Shawn descend the stage and sway over to the server's station at the end of the bar. By the time Sonny Shawn delivered the next round of drinks, Mrs. Rich's id so possessed her that she leaned over in her seat as if she had cramps and rocked like a lusting lunatic.

The DJ fired up the music and KC and The Sunshine Band sang, "Do a little dance, make a little love." The lid on Mrs. Rich's id flew away. She was out of her seat. "I wanna daaance," she declared, lifting her arms. "I never seen so many pretty men."

"Knock yourself out," Doris said, pausing from her machinations with Professor DeMint.

On the dance floor, partners seemed interchangeable and everybody smiled as Mrs. Rich curtseyed, do-si-doed, promenaded, and sang along with KC, her long skirt swishing and her torpedoes at the ready.

Doris opened her purse and looked down at the scissors inside. Professor DeMint rested her hand upon Doris's. "I got your back," she said.

Doris reached for her crutches. DeMint reached for her drink.

DeMint: "Valorize the now. But remember, there is no definitive narrative trajectory."

"Bingo."

When she saw her mother leave the dance floor, Doris disappeared into the crowd.

"Where's Doris?" Mrs. Rich said, wiping the sweat from her face before reaching for her drink.

"In the Now," DeMint said. Mrs. Rich detected a hint of sadness in the woman's voice.

"Meeee too," Mrs. Rich said waving for Shawn to bring another round. "Where's your husband?" she asked. A dark melancholy had descended upon the professor.

"There is no definitive narrative trajectory," she whispered. Then, "Which one?"

"How many husbands you got?" Mrs. Rich asked, her simmering id oozing lust as Sonny Shawn weaved a slinky path through the crowd to their table.

"I like your dress," Shawn said to Mrs. Rich. "You light up the place."

"I like them pants. You light up my life!" Mrs. Rich said in her most lascivious tone.

"You're sweet," said Shawn.

As Sonny Shawn turned to walk away, Mrs. Rich fell into a loud and off-key rendition of Debbie Boone's one hit. "Yooooou liite up my liiiiife!" Their server turned and blew her a kiss.

"Damn, I'm horny; I can't remember the last time I had any," Mrs. Rich said in a voice intended for anyone to hear. She reached for the fresh drink. "You were telling me about your husbands. How many you got?"

"None." The professor had become maudlin. She drank. "I've had four."

"At oncet?" Mrs. Rich joked. She had become drunk. She leaned in confidentially. "I've had me a three-some, though. You?"

"I've had a high school sweetheart husband, a book salesman husband, a truck driver husband, and a journalist husband. But I had 'em one at a time."

"Duhhh!" Mrs. Rich winked. "Only takes one man to have a three-some—or none," she purred. "You got you some learning to do, sister. Pull your chair up close."

***

BONUS TIP: Go for the slam dunk.

FRANK AND DORIS

The cheap dressing room door was shut, but it was so warped Doris could see him through a gaping crack. Frank sat before a mirror in the blond wig, mascara brush in one hand and eyeliner pencil in the other. Doris opened her purse and hooked the scissors with her pinky, then gripped her crutch. The door was unlocked.

Frank made last-minute touches to his eyes and reached for the powder to lighten his complexion and narrow his neck. He was looking into his giant makeup bag when he heard the door shut behind Doris.

"Hello," he said, not looking up from the bag. "I knew you'd be here; you were sitting up front."

"How'd you know I'd be here?"

He saw the scissors before he saw the look on her face. He spoke to the glistening, razor sharp blades. "This is a small town of ignorant people, Doris, but enough of them read that—"

"I'm here to settle a score."

"Well, if it's my testicles you want, you'd be doing me a favor."

"I'm here to cut out your heart."

Frank looked down at Barbara Streisand's breasts. "I wish you could. If you can find anything left of a heart in there, it's all yours for the taking."

Doris swung her leg forward, then gripped the scissors.

"I didn't know it was you at the bingo game," Frank said in a soft, steady voice. "I have an attorney on retainer. When you own a bingo parlor and a joint like this, you get sued every week. I didn't know until I read the papers." He reached into a bottom drawer.

"Don't you do it!" Doris screamed, leaping forward, scissors flying.

Frank froze, then slowly raised his sad eyes to hers.

"I hate you! I hate you!" Doris screamed over and over until she was emptied out.

Frank turned, exposing his chest to her. "If I had one, it would be about here." He touched a spot above his left breast. Slowly he lifted his hand from the dresser drawer. He held a white envelope. "Here's your five thousand."

"It's not about the money anymore." The scissors felt heavy as an anvil.

"I know." He reached for his red heels and spoke into the mirror. "We have to live for something, even if it's—this. Sometimes it ain't easy." Frank stood and laid his hand on Doris's shoulder. "Me, I live to give birth to a star. Pathetic as it sounds, it's the only happiness I got." He looked her in the eye, dropped his hand. "I'm sorry. About everything." Then he walked past her, down the dark hall.

Doris stood in the shadows near the back of the stage looking over the crowd. KC and the Sunshine Band were singing "That's the way, uh-huh, uh-huh, I like it," and the room was electric with happy faces. Their table was empty. Certainly a few minutes with her mom would be enough to send professor DeMint running for cover, and perhaps the Sunshine song had reminded Mrs. Rich of her Christian calling. Either way, Doris was alone, in a gay bar, in a small South Carolina town.

As smiling, sweaty dancers moved around her with care, Doris paused at her table just as the song wound down. A thumping version of YMCA began, and when she looked up at the line of dancers, Doris spotted Mrs. Rich and Professor DeMint shoulder to shoulder, flailing their arms, forming drunken hieroglyphics of the song's title. "Spell check!" somebody shouted and everybody laughed.

When the song ended, the lights faded at once. From the darkness offstage, Frank sang the opening lines of A Star Is Born. Dancers fell into each other's arms, and Mrs. Rich laid her head on Professor DeMint's shoulder. Their eyes closed in unison.

Alone in the blinding spotlight, Frank reached and clutched and sang every word as if it were true. When the song was over, the dimly lit room seemed suspended in time; the bodies swayed, close and warm, and nobody wanted it to end.

The opening notes of Unchained Melody began. Doris sensed a hand at her shoulder, then the crutches falling away. She felt strong, steady arms that lifted her into the fold, securely to Frank. And now their chests rose and fell in unison, their breasts coming together in little fish kisses.

"Place your foot on top of mine," he said. "I'll lead." And he did. "Just give it up."

And she did. When she opened her eyes, she and Frank were dancing beside Mrs. Rich and Professor DeMint, whose eyes never opened.

And when the song ended, another one began.

Somebody Wants Somebody Dead

I kill that second somebody. I don't know the person who wants the killing done, and they don't know me. The guy who's getting whacked usually deserves it. He's hated by more than one person, believe me. I don't do domestic cases.

The process starts with the Sunday New York Times. That's all you need to know about that. Here's the key. A string of numbers, a code. Could be something like this: 61595115230. Translation: June 15, Interstate 95, exit 115, 2:30 in the afternoon. The sequence of numbers changes, of course, but the information always falls in that order. When you come off the exit, there's gonna be a fast food hamburger place on the right. There's gonna be a hamburger bag beside the telephone booth outside. There's gonna be a sum of money—standard rate up-front fee—a message, and a telephone number inside the bag. Sometimes the message has special directions, like "Make it matter." Or "Bonus-eligible." You'll also find the details for the hit, a photo, place of work, home address, and any additional info to make sure things go smoothly. The person who hires the hit never knows exactly when it's gonna be made. And the whack-ee of course never sees it coming—unless the contract calls for it.

Surprise, surprise.

At the end of the job, there's a second string of numbers and a second hamburger bag. This one holds cash money, I'm not saying how much but plenty.

That, roughly, is how it's done.

For obvious reasons, I'm a man who doesn't like winding up on the wrong end of surprises. I'm guessing you probably don't either. But there's always room for misdirection, miscalculation, misunderstanding. So to eliminate any chances for surprises, I'll go ahead and tell you how this one turns out. Listen up: This all ends with me getting arrested in New Orleans for running around drunk and naked with hundred dollar bills taped to my body. Not what I'd planned.

Surprise, surprise.

***

My girlfriend Dana and I were sitting in the stands at Turner Field watching the Braves make a monkey of the Mets, a-gain. I've invited Dana along for cover and because it sometimes takes a few days—I'm not saying how many—to get the hit done, and also because I think I'm in love with her. She knows nothing about what I do, or she didn't at the time.

What she didn't know and what you may not have figured out yet is that the work is in the preparation. Humans are creatures of habit, in case you didn't know. Once you've got a person's routine, the rest is so easy that if I told you you wouldn't sleep so well. Before this thing I'm gonna tell you about happened, when it was time for me to earn my money, what I'd tell Dana is that I'm gonna run down to the 7-11 for a six-pack. Back in twenty minutes. That's what I'm thinking as we sit at Turner field.

So here I am on the first base side of the infield with tall, skinny Dana with great big tits and a laugh I really like. We'd started drinking at this restaurant called The Psycho-Deli, and now we were in the seventh inning and Mike Piazza is at bat, and I'd just ordered us another beer. Piazza hits one a mile high but not very deep. Dana and I stand and shout, "Cat shit, cat shit." We've been doing that all day, even when our own guys hit a pop fly.

Dana had started hosing up cocaine in the bathroom at The Psycho-Deli, and by now she's living for fly balls. We sat down after Andruw Jones retired Piazza and waited for the next batter. I glanced down at Dana's feet, which looked like Mr. Ed going through his multiplication tables, then checked my watch.

"Look," Dana said, extending her pointer finger, "a Chihuahua doing the wave."

"Drink up," I said. "Let's get out of here."

"I don't want to," Dana said looking back to the field. "I want to watch them wear those pants."

"Gotta go," I said.

"Cat shit," she said.

In the van, Dana put in her favorite CD, Jackie K and the Plastic Hearts. She tilted her head forward so that her long black hair fell over her face and sang Brain Bondage, yelling the words down into the floorboard. She looked over at me, gave me a wired smile. She really is my kind of girl.

***

Everything was going fine. Nobody on I-285 was on a mission from God to run me over, the afternoon was cooling down, and Dana was resting back with her eyes shut behind her sunglasses, singing with the Plastic Hearts.

I'm thinking about the special request that came with the Atlanta hit. The message in the hamburger bag had said, "Up close and personal." If you understand my line of work, you can translate. In case you don't, this is what a message like that means. First, every client wants a clean kill. Meaning there's nothing that connects the victim with the client. For that there is a fixed price. But let's face it, if I want to nail you with a scope or an explosive device, you never even feel it, right? Sometimes somebody wants you to feel it, and they are willing to pay a bonus if I can prove that my mark was fully cognizant of what was about to happen before it happened. Got it? Now, one piece of advice: If anybody offers you photos or tape recordings or videos as proof of purchase, run like hell. You got an amateur, one who'll be some gorilla's prom date when he gets to the big house. In this particular case, the bonus offered for "Up Close and Personal" was equal to the original selling price. For that kind of money, a client deserves something classy. I'd settled on gluing the guy's top teeth to the bottom ones. It was original, I thought, and way too good not to show up in the coverage.

So Dana and I stop at Rite Aid Drugs. I hand her a coupon I'd cut out of the newspaper for the Cap & Crown Cement, tell her the coupon's for toothache medicine, knowing that she's too wired to know the difference, and hand her a twenty.

"Come with me," she says.

"I'm gonna wait here. My tooth hurts."

"If you'll come with me, I'll buy you some rubbers," she purrs.

I put my hand up to my make-believe aching jaw. Dana opened her door, then looked back as she was getting out. "I might have something," she said in a sing-songy little girl's voice. "And if I do, you might cat shit." She waltzed toward the door of the drugstore. The woman's got a walk on her. You'd never guess she worked in a funeral home. She's a cosmetologist.

What I know is that drugstores have video cameras, and once the hit is done, the cops are maybe gonna be looking for a guy who's bought dental adhesive. A guy, not a girl, surely not one who pays with a coupon. If you saw the way Dana moves, you'd know there ain't nothing about Dana that could be mistaken for a guy. While she's inside, I make good use of the time.

There is this thing that professional athletes do called "projection," where they envision themselves hitting a Randy Johnson fast ball, or chipping a golf ball like Tiger Woods, or seeing the tennis ball before it comes over the net. I do the same in my work. I rehearse the hit. These things, done correctly, are always very, very simple. One piece of advice here. Somebody offers you some James Bond scenario for doing somebody, you stop, drop and roll, cause you got an amateur on your hands.

My guy, he looked maybe mid-fifties in the picture, professional CEO type, didn't pose much of a challenge. I'd be in my swim trunks and sweatshirt in the restaurant of the Peachtree Plaza Hotel at five-fifteen in the morning behind my newspaper, having coffee and reading about the Braves mopping up the Mets, a-gain. Mr. X passes me on his way to swim his twenty laps, which he does every morning. When he's done we ride up on the elevator, get off together, him first, me a safe distance behind. Once he has the plastic key in the door, I'd say, "Excuse me, did you lose this?" I'd hold up my watch and walk up to him. When his eyes go to the watch—and believe me they always do—I'd put the Heckler & Koch 9mm in his face. I know that's not how you see it on TV. On TV, they just walk up and put the pistol behind the guy's ear. But believe it or not, TV is not real. Do that in real life and you get trouble. You get somebody who's been surprised from behind, and you don't know what they might do. Unpredictable is what you don't want. Let them see you coming, give them something to distract their eye, then point a gun in their face and they forget they've got a mouth to talk with. They become trained pets. In fewer than five seconds, Mr. X and I are in his room. I do not speak. I see to it that he doesn't either. I have him lie spread-eagle and face up on the bed. You don't want him wondering what's going on behind his back. There is a pattern to this operation, I hope you know.

So I'm sitting in the Rite Aid parking lot with my eyes closed, watching all this, projecting, seeing the inside of the room, where the furniture is, where his bags are, whether or not the drapes are pulled. I lift my hand and rub my fingers like I'm tightening a nut onto a bolt, a signal that I want his money. If he's like the rest, he'll open his mouth to tell me where it is. That's when I cock the pistol and put a finger to my lips. From now on, he knows that we're dealing strictly in sign language. He points, and I open his wallet and take out the cash. Not that I need it. What I need is for him to think robbery is the motive. He don't know me. I don't know him. What's to tell him different? This all requires less than sixty seconds.

I reach inside the pocket of my swim trunks for the dental adhesive. He sees me unscrew the top. Then I motion for him to sit up. I hold the gun to his head and tuck one of his hands, then the other, palms down, under his ass. Next, I take a step back and give him a look that says I'll kill him if he moves his hands. Then I put the barrel of the gun under his nose and press lightly, while with the other hand I press down on his chin. He catches on quick. I apply the adhesive, top and bottom, then push the barrel up under his chin with just enough pressure to make sure the glue holds.

The rest is strictly by the book.

The hit will go down in the morning. The information I've been given says that he has reservations for a late-night flight to Hawaii. I've called the airport to double-check this information. It is correct. Which means that if I make the hit, say around six in the morning, nobody either in the hotel or in Hawaii is gonna start looking for him for at least fifteen hours.

What I don't realize is that fifteen hours after the hit, I'll be standing in a New Orleans jail with two black eyes, drunk, and naked except for the hundred dollar bills taped to me. Dana will show up with a Justice of the Peace. He asks me if I take her to be my wife. I mutter, "Giddy-up," and when he repeats the question to her she answers, "Umm-bobba maw-maw."

When I open my eyes, I see Dana walking across the Rite Aid parking lot in her tight black slacks and red tank top. There's something about a tall, skinny girl with knockers, something about the mechanics of motion. I can watch it for hours. After Dana gets back to the car, I look in the Rite Aid bag and count my change.

"You didn't use the coupon," I say. "Why didn't you use the coupon?"

"So?" she says.

"I went to the trouble to cut out that coupon, a dollar-off coupon."

"Oops, I guess I made a mistake," she said. "I guess I made a mistake and I didn't cat shit."

"I gave you the fucking coupon. I put the coupon in your fucking hand."

Dana opens her palm, and I see a small plastic bottle the size of my thumb.

"What's that?" I said. She showed it to me. It was called Sweet Breath.

She raised one arm then the other, squeezing a drop of breath freshener under each.

"I picked up something for myself," she said. "And for you."

I looked at the receipt.

"You stole this, didn't you? You shoplifted that stuff didn't you?"

She lifted one arm. "Taste it," she said.

"They have surveillance cameras in there," I said. "They've got you on tape."

"Lick it," she said.

A woman with spirit, with a little fire, I've always been attracted to that kind. But in my line of work there's no room for stupid mistakes, like shoplifting. A brain surgeon makes a careless move and snips out the piano lessons, his insurance company gets sued. I make a mistake, I got no insurance, I get hard time.

So Dana and I are having some words on the way back to the Day's Inn.

"You are soooo anal," she says.

"I ask you to do a simple favor, to make a simple fucking purchase. I give you a coupon and the money."

"And what's this shit about the coupon. Cutting coupons? Now that's some anal gay shit."

"The receipt will show the savings," I said. "There is a record of it."

"You are sooo fucked up."

"I just like doing things right."

"Yeah, well I can tell you one thing you won't be doing at all."

"Fuck you," I said.

"You're not only anal, you're deaf, too, you tight ass toothache fag."

That's probably enough to give you an idea of the direction this conversation was headed. We went back and forth like this until we got to the hotel, both of us yelling and screaming.

Since I'm explaining things, let me give you a little piece of advice. When a woman gets to the point Dana's at, all red-faced, her hands flying around as she screams at you, when she hyperventilates to catch enough breath to string together all the obscenities that are elbowing one another to force their way out, let me tell you what not to do. First, you can call her any name you would logically call a man. You can call her a shithead, a motherfucker, even a cocksucker. You can call her a bitch. You can probably get by with calling her a whore, provided the argument isn't sexual. But just remember this. She can call you a pussy, but you cannot, under any circumstances, call her a cunt. Which is what I did.

So now we're in the hotel room, and Dana first thing turns up the air conditioning full blast. Understand she's not saying anything, because it is her prerogative to shift from bully to brutalized woman in the time it takes to say the C word. So now she's acting all hurt and shit, the coke's left nothing but a mean streak in her, she's pacing like she's about to explode, and she's turned the air up to super cold.

Then she strikes back.

She sits on the bed and strips down her black slacks and flings off the red tank top so that now she's wearing only her panties, and she's finding every excuse to walk between me and SportsCenter, her perfect breasts riding as high as any you'll ever see; and her back is thin and long and settles into her hips, which are narrow, like I like them, and she's in those sheer red bikini panties that don't really hide anything.

I know when the game is over, so I say in a very civil voice, "Look, Dana." She slams the bathroom door. I hear the shower. A few minutes later, after the highlights of the Braves kicking some Mets ass, I try the door. It's locked. I watch until the replays come around again. The shower's still running. I knock. She doesn't answer.

She comes out wearing only a towel around her waist, tiny beads of water like diamonds in all the right places.

"Are you gonna shower?" she says, "Or are you going to dinner smelling like the shit you really are?"

I pretend I didn't hear the second half. "I thought we'd order out," I said. "I have to get up early to run an errand."

"Do what you want," she said, taking the small bottle of Sweet Breath from her purse. "I'll be dining out." Then she holds the small plastic bottle an inch or two above her bare breast, right in the middle of the dark brown circle, allows just one drop of the sweet nectar to fall, then turns and looks me in the eye as she passes the Sweet Breath above the other nipple. She looks down at the spot where the next drop will land and slowly presses her fingers together.

***

We have a very quiet and overpriced dinner at some place in Underground that is decorated with autographed photos of second-rate movie stars. The steaks are overcooked and the salads come sopping with dressing when I ordered it on the side. But the tables are small and the candlelight perfect. I order Dana a glass of red wine. I never drink the night before I work.

After dinner, I order her another glass of the Merlot and then an Amaretto. By the time it comes, we're holding hands. She's wearing a low-cut black dress and heels, and her hair and makeup are perfect. She's a cosmetologist. The events of the afternoon are seeping into faraway pools. She curls the top of her foot under the back of my calf, and I feel the electricity race up the inside of my leg and light up my circuits. She leans over the small table and whispers to me. I smell her sweet breasts.

"Let's make a night of it," she says. "I'm feeling a kink coming on."

I lift her hand and kiss it.

"How's about tomorrow night?" I say. She pulls her hand away. "Tell you what," I say. "After my breakfast appointment, we'll catch a flight to New Orleans. We'll get as kinky as you can imagine."

"You wouldn't know kink if it kicked you in the ass," she says, crossing her arms, deepening the cleavage. "You are such a pussy," she says.

I think the "C" word, but my lips don't move.

My watch says ten o'clock, and I'm looking for a place near Cleveland Street to park the van. Dana has requested I take her to a comedy club for a nightcap. I'm already off my usual work schedule.

The place is nearly packed, but two women are leaving just as we walk in. We take their table right up front.

"We have time for one drink," I tell Dana. "I gotta work in the morning."

Dana looks up at our waitress and then over at me.

"I'll have a vodka-tonic," she says, "and my girlfriend here will have a double vodka-tonic." The waitress walked away.

"Fuck yourself," I say.

"I intend to," she says.

The waitress set the drinks on the table. Dana reached for the double in front of me. She buried her finger in the vodka, stirred, lifted the dripping finger and slid it into her mouth up to the knuckle, then slowly withdrew it.

"I just cunt finger you out," she said.

The lights went up, and a woman in her late twenties wearing baggy brown pants and a bulky black sweater slouched at the back of the stage, her hands clasped behind her. Her light brown hair was pulled back into a ponytail. She wore winged glasses and looked down at the floor. For a few seconds, you'd have thought she maybe missed her bus.

She timidly skated up to the microphone and whispered, "I like it up the ass." Then she squenched up her face so that her eyes were slits and showed all her teeth. Everybody laughed. Dana reached for her drink.

The comic's anal sex jokes divided neatly into three varieties. She liked it up there because she was a dutiful wife and men were so sexually incompetent. She liked it up there because as a victim of social oppression she really had no choice because men are so insensitive. She liked it up there because as a liberated woman she was entitled to sexual gratification and men were so inadequate. She mixed and matched. Dana was laughing her ass off.

Near the end of her routine, the woman sat with her legs dangling from the stage right in front of us. Dana knocked off the last of the vodkas.

"You know, ladies?" she whispered confidentially. "When he snuggles up behind you?" She laid over on her side with her back to us, talking over her shoulder.

"Uh-huh," Dana answered.

"And you think he's going to Atlanta, but he'd headed for...Decatur?"

"Uh-huh," Dana said.

I'm looking over at her now.

"And he first introduces Winkie to your Twinkie?" She pointed at her butt.

"Oh, yes," Dana says to her.

I'm looking from Dana to the comedian, then back at Dana.

"And he gives you the... fudge nudge?"

"Ooooh, yes!"

"Do you know what to do, ladies?"

"You betcha," Dana shouted over the laughter. The comic was working the timing.

"You give him the kink wink!" The whole place was laughing. "You know," she said. She pulled her baggy pants up her crack, and clenched and unclenched her cheek muscles like a winking eye. The place was howling. The comic, who said her name was Rhonda Reardon, stood, shouted goodnight and bounded off the stage.

"Are you ready to go?" I said. Dana lifted her empty glass, sized up its contents, and set it back down.

"I rectum so," she said.

Back in the van, Dana turned on the radio. An old song called Elvira was on.

"Did you ever watch Elvira on TV?" she said. The vodka had kicked in, taking the edge off.

"Who?" At this time of night, I'm on the lookout for Georgia State Troopers.

"That vampire diva that did the late night horror movies on the Atlanta station."

"I don't know who you're talking about."

"Elvira. I looooved Elvira, all dressed in black leather and not afraid to show a little cleavage. I wanted to be Elvira. You could just tell she got whatever the hell she wanted. I looooved Elvira." she said.

It was a little after midnight when we got back to the room. Dana went into the toilet, and I set the clock for 3:45. I didn't like the way this was all shaping up. You need a very clear head in my line of work, a very clear head. I undressed and got into bed. I was drifting off when I heard Dana come out. She was singing softly, "El-VIR-ruh, El-VIR-ruh." I watched as she crossed the room with only the faint light from outside to carve the outline of her nakedness.

She lay with her back to me. I put my hand on her hip and traced its contour up her long waist, over her stomach, up to her breast. Any man in America would have done the same.

"El-VIR-ruh," she sang in a whisper. She lifted my hand and brought my fingers up to her mouth. She pressed back against me. You know what happened next.

Dana returned my wet fingers to her breast. "My heart's on fire-ruh for El-VIR-ruh," she said breathily. "Giddy-up, umm-bobba maw-maw." She reached back and pulled me closer.

I looked over at the clock. There are no minor leagues in my line of work.

"Can you spell 'kink'?" I whispered in her ear.

"Giddy-up," she purred.

I plotted my course to Decatur.

"I've got a sweet tooth," I said softly.

"Umm-bobba maw-maw."

"I'm craving some Twinkies."

I introduced the kink and awaited a wink.

Dana's elbow struck my nose with such force that my cupped palm was overflowing with blood when I staggered into the bathroom.

I took two extra-strength P.M. aspirins and after a while fell asleep breathing through my mouth.

***

In my dream, I was drowning in arctic waters. The alarm went off. When I swam to the icy surface, I discovered that Dana was gone. And that she had taken the blanket and bedspread. And that she'd turned the air up full blast. And that she had glued my teeth together.

***

I dressed and walked out to the van, which was parked on an incline across from the room and far from any bright lights. I discovered that it was unlocked, which wasn't like me, a guy thoughtful enough to have disconnected the interior lights. You can't be too careful in my line of work. I released the emergency brake and coasted to the street, then started the engine and switched on the headlights. Even with my swollen nose and glued teeth, I could smell the scent of Sweet Breath inside the van.

I drove around the block once looking for Dana, thinking maybe she'd had time to cool off, that maybe she might be coming back to me. But it was too dark to see much. I looked down at my watch.

By the time I made the interstate, I was seriously projecting. The Cap & Crown Cement that was gonna double my money had only doubled my problems.

At 5:15 I was sitting in the Peachtree with my newspaper and a cup of coffee I couldn't drink when Mr. X walks by with his towel and swim cap. Despite the lack of sleep and the throb in my nose, I am razor sharp. I have shifted into professional high gear. Even the fat nose, I think, has a purpose. I don't really look like myself.

At exactly 5:45 I see my mark headed back in my direction. I put my watch in my left palm and lift my towel, which holds the Heckler & Koch 9mm, and begin to fold my paper as he passes. He presses the button at the elevator, the door opens, and we both step inside. I move behind and angle my body away from him.

Now if you've been paying attention you'll remember that once he gets the plastic key in the door, I hold up my watch and say, "Excuse me, did you drop this?" That and maybe a quick "Open the door" are my only lines. Minimum movement, minimum sound, minimum risk. Only guess what? Dana has glued my teeth. So it's improv time. When I see the key in his hand, I pick up my pace and dangle my watch up high. "Excuse me" comes out "sqooooooooooo muu," but he looks around anyway, and I can tell at once that the guy's half blind by the way he tilts his head and crinkles his eyes at the watch. This is gonna be too easy, I think for a second. He bends forward to see what's in my hand and I present him with the 9mm.

Then this shit happens. The fucker faints. Falls out like a bag of fertilizer. I've got to hold the pistol on him, feel for the key, wait for the blinking green light, open the fucking door, and get the sack of shit inside.

I've got my foot against the open door and a good grip on one wrist when I look up. Dana, in that black low-cut dress, purse, and heels is watching from the open elevator door. She steps forward. For a second we just stand where we are. I'm looking at her. She's looking at me, giving me this perfect chick-flick look, her eyes all watery and shit. Then her hand slowly rises and her fingers open like she's making an offering. I see the Cap & Crown Cement in her palm.

I leave him on the floor just inside the door and take Dana by the arms and stand her up like a mannequin on the far side of the bed.

"Where's the six-pack?" she says.

"Shhhhhhh!"

Rip Van Winkle moves and I rush over just in time to put the 9mm in his mouth when he opens it. I lift him by the arm, then motion for him to lie on the bed.

Because I'm a professional, I always carry two pairs of gyno rubber gloves with me to work. They're rolled up in my towel, which I'm about to unroll on the dresser, when Mr. Tomorrow's Obituary decides it's his turn to talk.

"What do—" he says. I raise the pistol an inch or two and take a step toward him. When he opens his eyes again, he sees me giving him the shush sign. From the corner of my eye, I see Dana cross her arms. She has a curious smile going. I'm unrolling the towel when Dana makes a move toward the chair. Out of instinct, I turn the gun on her. She stops in her tracks. I see her lovely chest rise and fall, see a rush of color, her eyes wide and bright. I'm feeling a little like a juggler on a tight wire.

This won't help you sleep any better on your summer vacation, but a hotel room is the perfect setting for my kind of work. Every one of them is a regular haystack of fibers and hair samples, except for the sheets. There's so much trace evidence that it becomes meaningless— that is if you have an ounce of sense and any degree of professional standards.

Mr. No Tomorrow is studying me hard as I pull on first one and then the other gyno glove. You can tell his eyes are bad. His nostrils flare and his breathing is labored. I'm thinking he might fall out again, but he doesn't. I raise my free hand and give him the old I'm-screwing-the-bolt-on-the-nut-give-me-your-money sign. But he's not buying it. Whatever the hell this guy's done, he knows he's going down for it.

"Fuck you," he says in a weak voice. I start over toward him. The cat's out of the bag, I'm thinking. No reason for the old bait and switch. "You guys are a bunch of pussies," he says, knowing he's about out of words.

Dana giggles. We both turn and look at her.

"You cunt," he says to her. I draw back the hammer, and he squeezes his eyes shut. Dana is charging toward him swinging her purse.

And on account of I'm a pro, I have a brilliant idea. I hold up my hand like a traffic cop, and lucky for me, Dana stops. The lust in her eyes has turned a fiery Agent Orange color. I give her a little smile that makes her tilt her head and draw her eyebrows together. I hand her the second pair of gyno gloves. She smiles at me again in that way I like.

It is a sexual act, the way she eases her hands into those gloves. "Giddy-up," she purrs in a breathy whisper. She works her hands all the way in, spreads her fingers wide, and then forms two tight fists. "Um-bobba Maw-maw." Mr. Deadman takes a deep breath and looks over at me with the pleading look of the slimy cocksucker he is.

I motion for Dana to step close. I lift the towel and lay it over my arm, take her by the hand, and lead her to the side of the bed. I place the muzzle of the 9mm against Mr. Lucky's right ear, and with my other hand reach for the top button of Dana's black dress. As the button is freed, she trembles. When I liberate the second one, she gently swoons. When I touch the third button, she pushes away my hand and takes over. She steps out of her dress.

Mr. Bye-Bye's goldfish eyes are darting from Dana to me. I motion for her to roll up the dress. When my rubber-gloved hand touches her bare, thonged behind, she looks over at me, and we are of one mind.

Dana disappears into the bathroom, and returns with the plastic wastebasket liner. She steps out of her heels, then strips off her bra and panties and tucks them and the dress into the liner.

She stands naked except for the rubber gloves.

I spread the towel on the edge of the bed where the soon-to-be-dead man is having his last look at a beautiful, naked woman. Dana sits on the towel. I open her purse. She runs her fingers up my thigh.

I slide the purse over. Dana reaches inside for her cosmetics.

This is another thing you probably didn't know. If somebody presses the barrel of a 9mm down on your skull, you won't open your eyes. So I stand over my day's work, giving Dana room, holding the pistol like a hand drill against the guy's noggin.

Dana begins with a thick yellow moisturizer. Next, she lifts a small brown glass bottle and mouths the word "foun-da-tion." She applies the pasty liquid with a graceful, delicate touch, then sits back and assesses. She reaches into her purse and brings out a light, translucent powder.

With a brush in her hand, she becomes another woman: still my Dana, but another woman too. She applies a second shade of powder in the center of the cheeks, and a third at the base of his jaw. With one pencil she lines his eyebrows, with another his eyes. My tall, skinny Dana is a pro. First rate.

"Ah lub hue," I whisper.

"Giddy-up," she whispers. She applies mascara to the lashes and eyebrows, highlighter on the cheeks. "My heart's on fire-ruh, I'm El-VIR-ruh."

She brushes on blush before adding a touch of blue shadow to the eyelids, and then paints on two shades of red lipstick.

Beautiful naked Dana, my Dana, sat back. She took a deep, lovely breath. I touched her face with my gloved hand. Looking up into my eyes, she kissed my finger. Then she turned and studied her canvas.

Dana drew in another slow, deep, meditative breath. Her long black hair fell back, and her eyes glowed soft and dark. After a time, she reached again for her brushes and pencils. When she was finished, she quickly packed the cosmetics into her purse, stood, and without a word, stepped into her panties.

Fully dressed, she stood in front of the mirror applying her own lipstick. She lifted her purse and reached for the towel, which she had rolled up inside the plastic liner. I held out the keys to the van.

***

The rest went strictly by the book.

***

Even before I reached the lobby doors, I heard the sounds of Jackie K. and the Plastic Hearts. Dana sat behind the wheel.

A few minutes later, as we approached the airport on I-285, I pointed to the exit sign, making sure Dana didn't miss it. The morning rush had already begun.

"Let's just drive to New Orleans," she said. She turned up the air a notch, and I curled up in the Day's Inn bedspread. "What's the hurry, huh?" She leaned over and gave my thigh a squeeze.

I woke when Dana took an exit just east of Birmingham and pulled in at a Rite Aid Drug store. "Think kink," she said smiling. I watched her walk. She returned with a new bottle of Sweet Breath and a thick roll of clear tape. She handed me the receipt and kissed my bruised cheek.

Soon after we entered New Orleans, she whipped into a shabby strip mall and double-parked in front of a rundown costume shop. At the shop door, she turned and blew me a kiss, then disappeared inside. I thought of the way she'd held the soft brushes and eyeliner pencils, her intense concentration, her stunning naked beauty.

When she tossed the plastic bag into the back, I saw a black, low-cut, Latex dress, a black wig, and I didn't know what else. "Vot ees the KIN-kiest ting voo can THINK of?" she said in a perfect vampire voice. Our eyes met.

"Twoo lub," I said.

We kissed, sort of. She tried to give me her sweet tongue. But you can imagine. Dana laughed and shifted down into drive. "We'll celebrate," she said, giving me her vampire's smile. "We'll celebrate your new bonus. We'll celebrate the highest form of kink—like you can't imagine."

***

Which explains why I was later arrested in the French Quarter for running around with two black eyes, mute, drunk and naked with hundred dollar bills taped to my body. Because the fact is I couldn't imagine the highest, kinkiest thing—true love. That is until I saw Dana on the other side of the cell bars, in that Latex dress and black wig, accompanied by a man I'd never seen.

When the Justice of the Peace said, "Do you take this woman," I muttered, "Giddy up." And when he said to her, "Do you take this man," Dana smiled at me and said, "Uhm bobba mau-mau" and passed a pair of my slacks between the bars.

Outside, we looked up at the dark clouds of a gathering storm and then out at the city of New Orleans, the city that was for a time ours. Dana took my hand, leading me in a direction we hadn't taken. She looked straight ahead then up at the dark sky. We walked for a while before she spoke.

"Surprise, surprise," she said.

Neighborhood Watch

The .22 rifle in the corner of the bathroom belonged to Jackson's wife, Terri. It had been there for five months, since early April. At first, Terri gently complained about the clutter, but she hadn't mentioned the rifle or the ammunition all summer. When she cleaned, she set the small black plastic box of bullets to the side along with the crystal bowl of apple-scented potpourri, then centered the box again on the back of the toilet when she was done. But now that September had come, she again asked Jackson about it.

"Put yourself in the mind of Lee Harvey Oswald," he said with a fetching smile.

The bathroom window overlooked their small backyard, where astilbe, hostas, wood ferns, and impatiens grew in the shade of the dogwoods and where purple petunias, white begonias, orange hibiscus, and red roses shimmered in the late summer light. Early every morning as he drank his first cup of coffee, Jackson toured their small garden and assessed the rodent damage.

In the afternoon after work, he and Terri had their drinks in the shade, praised the day's growth, delighted in the day's blooms, and cursed the squirrels.

"But you can't kill them," Terri said, setting her glass on the patio table.

"You're talking in that Thumper voice again," Jackson said smiling, referring to the childlike lyrical inflection Terri affected when she spoke of small animals. "Think of them as rats with fluffy tails," Jackson said. "They kill our babies."

Every spring Terri and Jackson studied the weather and shared intimate, anticipatory conversations about what to plant and when the odds no longer favored frost. At the farmers market, they carefully selected a rainbow of flats and devoted their weekends to the infant flowers—first digging, then working the black soil with their fingers, stirring in a little cow manure and fertilizer before cuddling and covering their roots. They called the small flowers their babies.

But the squirrels invaded, appropriating the soft, fertile places, uprooting and tossing aside the tiny plants, then burying pecans from the neighbors' trees.

"Well, if you kill something, I don't want to know, okay? Just don't tell me."

Two houses over, a car door slammed shut. A small child was crying.

"Shut up," a man shouted. "Or I'll burn your ass."

Jackson and Terri exchanged looks.

"I can't stand that," Terri said.

"Somebody ought to kick his ass," Jackson said.

The child, no more than four years old, wore a faded pink dress. Her rust colored hair fell in thick ringlets over small dirty hands pressed hard against her eyes. She turned, head down, half folded at the waist, and slowly walked stiff-legged away from the man, down the dusty drive.

"I saw the sign was down," Jackson said to his wife. "Be grateful it wasn't that one they bought." He nodded toward the sign in front of the house next door.

Two houses over, the girl's father stood in the shadow of his slanted garage with his back to them, smoking.

***

Jackson set down his razor and lifted the bathroom window a few inches, enough to get the barrel of the rifle out. The squirrels did their damage in the early mornings and late afternoons. Two fluffy cats, one orange and white the other black, lay in the bed of red and white impatiens.

"They have four children," Terri said. Jackson turned. Terri was drying her hair in a towel.

"And soon, two dead cats," Jackson said.

"The oldest looks to be about eight, the youngest maybe three or four."

Jackson looked again. The cats sat sphinx-like, their noses tilted up. They were waiting for the squirrels.

"You can't shoot somebody's cats," Terri said.

"They're in the flowers. They'll make a sandbox of the place."

"You can't shoot somebody's cats," she said.

At the corner of Hampton and West Broad, two blocks from home, Jackson slowed for the stop sign when he saw the new neighbor's youngest girl standing alone on the sidewalk in a two-piece swimsuit that would fit inside a teabag. At first he thought she might be lost. He looked both ways, then looked both ways again with a rising panic, sensing that the child was about to cross. He lowered his window as he pulled through the intersection and pushed his face forward, hoping she would recognize him.

"Are you okay?" he said. She seemed not to hear him. "You shouldn't be this far from home." When she looked up at him, he realized she wasn't lost at all. Crossing her arms, she turned to her left and then to her right like a sentry.

"You can't tell me what to do," she said, lifting her chin a notch.

"This is dangerous. Go home."

He wanted to say, Does your mother know where you are? But he knew his question would be wasted. She turned her back and held her ground. "I live right there," Jackson pointed, "and when I park my car, I'm going to come out to the street and watch you walk home." A car stopped behind him. The driver tilted her head out of the window, suspiciously assessing Jackson as he spoke to the almost naked little girl. "I'm gonna be watching," he said again. He pressed the gearshift and eased off the clutch, glancing back into his mirror. The girl stuck out her tongue and wagged her tiny hips.

When he pulled into his drive, he confronted a plastic tricycle with a large black wheel in front and two tiny ones in back. Elbows as sharp as bats' wings jutted up from the grips. Protruding over the plastic handlebars were concave eyes set in a V-shaped face and surrounded by a large head with hair the color and texture of a cocklebur. The boy was maybe eight years old.

Jackson sat for a second with the engine idling, waiting, but the boy didn't budge. Lifting his foot off the brake, Jackson allowed the car to ease toward the tricycle. The kid didn't move. Jackson laid his thumb lightly on the horn. A good scare would wipe away that sneer. But instead, Jackson shifted into park. The kid slid his index finger knuckle-deep up his nose and gave it a slow dig. Jackson felt the blood rush. He opened his door and stepped out. He started toward the kid.

"You can't play in my drive," he said. The boy wouldn't look at him. "It's dangerous. I might pull in here and not see you." The boy turned the wheel. "Stay in your own yard," he said to the boy's back. The squat little kid pushed with his feet and crossed the adjacent yard with the speed and agility of a Palmetto bug.

Looking down at his house key, Jackson started for the door. Then he remembered the boy's sister in the tiny bikini. When he got to the street, an old Cadillac with smoked windows and no hubcaps was peeling away from the stop sign at Hampton. The girl was nowhere in sight.

***

Terri filled two glasses with ice and made drinks. She handed her husband a bourbon.

"They have dogs too, mongrels, one black the other brown. There was a piece of mail for Graham in ours today. When I took it over to him, he said their dogs killed his cat." Jackson and Terri shared a look. Then she smiled.

"Hey, big guy," Terri said, reaching for Jackson's hand, "Let's sit outside."

The cats had slept in the impatiens and scratched out small mounds in the petunias. Jackson and Terri stood over the purple flowers, having their drinks without speaking. Terri reached for his hand again, giving it a soft squeeze.

"They're back," Terri said in that pleasant childlike voice, looking up. They stepped to a clearing. Above were two Red-tailed hawks, a mated pair that had returned for the past four summers, making their nest within sight. With the grace of a maestro's hands they sailed and swooped, landing now in the top of the tall pecan tree next door.

"Do you think a hawk would kill a cat?" Jackson said. He was looking back at their flowerbed.

"I wish," said Terri in her little girl's voice.

***

Outside, a car horn blew.

"Terri?" Jackson called as he walked toward her. "What happened?"

She stood in front of the car, hands on her hips. The engine was still running, and the smell of hot rubber drifted toward Jackson as he neared her. The car was overheating. She was looking out, across their yard.

"I don't believe those kids," Terri said, nodding toward the neighbors' house. "When I started up the drive, I thought one of their dogs was in our yard again. I saw something moving in the camellias. When I told the kids to get out, they just hunkered down. Finally I took the older girl by the arm. 'You can't play in there,' I said; 'you can't play in my shrubs.' 'It's where we go to hide,' the oldest said. 'It's our place,' she said. 'Where we hide from the monsters.' Then the three of them just stood there in the drive with their arms crossed, wearing a smirk I wanted to slap off their dirty faces. They just stood there."

On the sidewalk up front, Jackson and Terri heard the sound of churning gravel. Knees pumping like pistons, elbows flared, the boy turned his dark eyes on them, then thrust his angular head over the plastic handlebars.

"When I told them to go home, the oldest put her hands on her hips. 'Piss on your flowers,' she said. Can you imagine? The child can't be six years old. Then they marched off. 'Piss on your old flowers,' she said again when they were off a ways. Then she looked right at me. She called me a bitch. Put her hands on her hips. 'Biiitch,' she said. I wanted to strangle her."

They looked over at the neighbor's yard as if the children lingered there, hiding, watching, and listening. A cool breeze lifted the dogwood leaves, and the autumn sunlight brought out the red tint that lay deep, waiting in them. Jackson smelled the rubber stench from the hot engine.

He looked at Terri, then pressed his palm gently against her back and rubbed small circles. "Want to make a drink and sit outside?" he said.

"No. I can't stand the sight of them."

***

They had eaten supper, and now they sat outside.

The Christmas tree lights they had hung like a canopy in the black cherry tree in the center of the patio had always seemed romantic to Terri. But now the tiny lights cast dim shadows on Jackson's face. She had watched her husband from the time she heard the low rumble of the neighbor's truck nearing.

"No, Jackson. Not after we've had drinks."

"I'll have a word," he said, rising from his chair.

"It's a conversation to have without drinks," Terri said. Jackson reached for his glass, drained it, set it gently on the table. Together they watched the headlights enter the garage, heard the engine shut down. Terri held out her hand to Jackson. He stepped past her.

"We could just call the police or something," she said.

Jackson walked from the canopy of tiny lights into the shadows. She heard the truck door shut.

The man stepped out of his garage into the hazy yellow porch light of his house.

From his rising anger, Jackson felt a kind of levitation, that feeling of the muscles in his thighs taking over. The neighbor started up the cement steps, his every joint fluid, as if his body were boneless, its mechanics the product of internal hydraulics.

Terri saw the man clearly now in the yellow porch light, his slinky-thin frame. She watched him reach for the door.

"Hey!" Jackson called from the shadows.

The man paused, slowly turning and lifting his head as if he'd suddenly picked up a scent.

Terri watched as her husband's form entered the outer circle of murky light.

"Hey," Jackson called again. "We got to talk."

The man pulled open the screen, then stopped. His head bent and swooped down serpent-like, to the left, toward Jackson, who looked up at him. Jackson's hands became fists. He jammed them into his back pockets as he leaned forward, waiting for his neighbor to step down.

Behind him, Terri's voice called from across the way. He looked back. She was standing in the soft halo of Christmas lights beside the patio table. She lifted her arms to him.

Then he heard the screen door bang shut.

A kind of electricity shot through him. He took the concrete steps in twos. He knocked twice, hard.

Terri called to him.

He waited. The orange and white fluffy tabby pressed itself against his ankle and slid against him. He felt the anger rising, spilling over. His mouth tasted of tepid water from a tin can. Jackson knocked again, this time with the meaty edge of his fist. He heard movement inside and a woman's voice. The kitchen door opened slowly like a heavy gate.

Through the silver wire screen mesh, a vague blue aura emanated from the massive, bovine woman. Jackson pulled opened the door. The blue light's source, a roaring TV, sat in the other room. The sallow broad figure in the faded black Mega Death sweatshirt and white spandex shorts slowly rotated, muttering in rising inflections, a combination stammer and gasp, an emphatic inaudible utterance without substance. An immense skull appeared half buried between her massive shoulders and its lidless bloated eyes seemed fixed upon the ceiling or something beyond. The woman began to sway from side to side. One fleshy hand slowly ascended as if she were grasping at a moment of rapture, while the other hand pressed hard against the side of her heavy jowls. Jackson drew a breath and felt his body shrink from her.

Then he saw the cell phone in her meaty palm.

"Look," he said.

Her bulbous eyes bent down on him. Then a wild look of exaltation seized her face as if that moment of rapture were upon her. "You bitch!" she screeched, looking down into the phone. She reached blindly toward him, her meaty fingers kneading the air. "Fuuuuck you!" she screamed into the cell. Jackson stepped back onto the porch, recoiling from her shadow.

Rotating slowly on her axis, the woman turned her back to him, lifted her foot like a trained elephant, and then hammered the door shut.

Jackson stood in the porch light, exposed.

He saw Terri standing beside the patio table under the faint tree lights, her hands tightly knotted under her chin. He took the steps slowly. As he crossed the dark yard, he suddenly felt a presence at his shoulder. Jackson stopped and looked back. At the glowing cosmic blue window, he saw the four children piled one over another like newborn moles and felt their black sightless eyes following him across the yard.

***

The first frost came early, the second week in October, taking them by surprise. Ordinarily, Jackson and Terri brought the hibiscus inside. With adequate sunshine and a little care they'd have blooms at Christmas. Now it was too late.

Wearing a sweater but no socks, Jackson poured his morning coffee. Outside, the impatiens drooped like tide-cast octopi, their runners fleshy and soft. Though green still, the petunias' purple blooms lay like small brown footprints. A cold breeze brought down the bruised-red dogwood leaves. He turned and looked at the neighbors' house. Their dogs had scavenged the trashcan again. On the far side of the yard, the top of a pizza box waved at him like a circus clown.

He would warm the car for Terri, that's what he'd do. She'd like that. He went inside for her car key.

"I have a teachers' meeting this afternoon, if you want to take something out for supper," she said, slipping on her coat.

"I guess it's time to put out the pansies, huh?" Jackson said.

"I don't know," Terri said. "I just don't know."

"Maybe just in the pots up front," he said.

"Maybe in the pots," she agreed.

After starting her car, Jackson poured their coffee as Terri packed the lunch he'd made for her.

"Have you seen the hawks?" he asked.

"I'm pretty sure they were here last year this time. Who knows?"

"Last year was different," Jackson said, handing her the plastic lunch bag.

He kissed her at the door.

As he dressed, Jackson watched clouds as black and ominous as lava oozing over the tree line to the west. He locked the back door and started for his car. He didn't hear the neighbor's truck pull in, only heard the door shut.

The man wore camouflage from head to foot. Plodding his way up the porch steps, he turned his eyes upon Jackson. He'd not bothered to wipe the brown and black paint from his face. On the barrel of the rifle slung down in his loose hand, Jackson saw the scope, as large as his forearm.

The man unlaced his heavy boots, pulled one off and dropped it on the porch. He was pulling off the second as Jackson jammed his key into the ignition.

***

By the weekend, October had returned. Terri and Jackson worked in short sleeves, raking and mulching.

"They're still here," Terri said. Jackson looked up. The two Redtails were gliding high. He and Terri stood close watching. The large birds tilted and swooped against the aqua sky, the popcorn clouds whiter still in the yellowing autumn light. Terri reached for Jackson's hand.

"There really is something calming about watching them, isn't there?" Jackson said. "Gliding, floating. That's how I want to come back."

"It's like looking up into a giant fish tank, isn't it?"

"You only get so many of these, huh?" Jackson said softly, pulling Terri against him.

Later, they sat at the patio table drinking iced tea, looking over their afternoon's work. The beds were freshly raked but bare.

"Well, what's the final verdict on planting pansies?" Jackson asked, watching as the orange and white cat waddled over to a dirty plastic milk jug at the foot of the neighbors' porch steps.

The squealing pitch of the woman's voice made it impossible for Terri or Jackson to decode her obscenities. When they looked over, they saw the fleshy arm shove the girl out onto the porch, then withdraw into the house. The child wore the faded pink dress and no shoes. She sat on the top steps, her shoulders folded, her face buried in her hands.

"I don't think so," said Terri. "I think we'll pass on planting pansies this year."

The thick orange and white cat lumbered cautiously up the steps toward the crying child. The girl sat motionless, her knees tight, head down. The cat neared the top step. Its swollen, pregnant body leaned slowly toward the child's bone-thin leg.

The girl's small foot struck the cat's belly with the speed and force of an angry cottonmouth. The cat toppled and spilled down three steps before finding its balance and waddling away like a frightened seal.

***

When the wind and rain let up, Terri stood at the kitchen window looking out at the bare dogwood. The circle of crimson leaves around the tree reminded her of a dry blood spoor. Every autumn she felt the dying season settle into her.

She found her gardening gloves on the back porch and walked to the garage for a rake. She stopped.

Inside, the three girls stood in a line, heads down, near the back of the garage where the door to the old pantry cabinet swung open. Their brother bowed on one knee in front of them, aiming a can of red spray paint at the oldest sister's shoes. He had already sprayed the sneakers of the two younger girls. On the cement floor, islands of red paint surrounded each of their tiny feet.

Terri pulled off her gloves and threw them down hard.

Later, she sat at the patio table in her sweater drinking hot coffee, waiting. She rose when she heard the familiar rumble of the black truck as it approached from the stop sign. She was standing in the center of his drive with her arms folded when the man pulled in.

"Where's your proof?" the man said.

Terri turned. The man followed at an uncomfortable distance. She glanced back twice on the short walk to her garage, finding that he shifted from her left to her right, then back again.

"What are you going to do about this?" They were both looking down at the white prints in the dried red circles.

"Kids is kids," he said. "What's the harm?"

"That's not good enough," Terri said. "They have no business—"

The man turned and walked away.

"That's not good enough!" Terri shouted at his back.

She had stood looking down at the three red islands, then stepped over to the boy. Taking the can from him, Terri felt his small wrist give when she squeezed it, felt strength enough to squeeze until the thin bone snapped. Now she wished she had.

She lifted a rake, then set it down, picked up her gloves and started inside. The man's voice called from across the way.

"Hey, you!"

The neighbor was standing on the porch waiting, holding up the boy's hand like a winning prizefighter's. When Terri looked over, he lifted the boy so that his left foot hardly touched and dragged the child like a heavy sack down the porch steps. A thick black belt in his left hand snaked behind. He didn't take his eyes from Terri's as he pulled the boy into view, then reached down to double up the belt. She hurried for the back door.

"This is what you get," the man shouted at her. "This is what you *get*."

Terri glanced back. The boy's small body arched, his eyes squeezed shut, and his mouth fell open like a newborn kitten's. His first scream was filled with air, and the pain had a name, as did his second and his third scream. Inside, Terri rushed to her bedroom window.

When she inched the curtains apart, the man's eyes were fully upon her, and now as the boy slowly orbited his father, the screams emptied of air though the boy's mouth gaped, until all that was left in him was a breathless, sucking hiss.

"*This* is what you get!" the man shouted.

***

"The car's still running hot," Terri said. "You said you'd fix it, but it's still running hot."

"I put in some antifreeze."

"You *said* you would fix it. It's still running hot." She made a tight knot of the ends of the plastic bag that held her lunch. "It's not safe to drive," she said, getting into her coat. "Fuckin' car."

Terri felt the crusty frosted grass under her feet as she walked toward the garage. Looking up, she saw the kid slumped and folded on the black tricycle, his hidden face buried inside the hood of a coat too big for him. She could see his breath. Terri looked away, down at the car keys in her hand.

"Hey!" the boy shouted in a thin, squawking voice. A white puff rose from the deep hood. Terri stopped and looked. "I'm gonna cut your neck off!" he shouted.

As soon as she stepped into the garage, she saw the deep sinuous gouge down the length of her car, from headlight to bumper.

"We should call the police," Jackson said, looking at the damage. The boy had disappeared. "For the insurance."

Terri just looked at him, then opened the door, started the car, and backed out without speaking.

***

The pistol was small and light. Jackson had inherited it. His dad had bought it for shooting snakes when he was bass fishing. It felt like a toy in Jackson's coat pocket now as he and Terri stood silently at the bedroom window waiting for headlights and sipping their second drink. Jackson hadn't said anything to Terri about the pistol. Neither of them spoke when Jackson left the room.

The neighbor was wearing his deer hunting clothes, and Jackson stepped between him and the man's truck, between the man and the rifle in the bed of the truck. He held his flashlight on the neighbor. "Let's have a look," the man said.

Jackson walked with his hand inside his coat pocket, uneasy that the man trailed a few steps behind weaving from side to side. Jackson pointed the light at the side of the scarred car.

"Where's your evidence?" the man said.

"I'll call the police," Jackson said.

The man chuckled. "Go call 'em."

"This is my wife's car."

The man bent over and began untying his heavy hunting boot. His face was hidden in the dark. Jackson stepped back. His fingers tighten on the pistol grips. "Like I said," the man spoke into the cement floor, "where's your evidence? Call 'em. You think they're gonna fingerprint a bunch of little kids?" He laughed again as he straightened up, his raised head appearing to lengthen his thin neck. "Tell me a jury is going to believe a kid would do such a thing?" He took another look at the damage, then turned and started away, slowly tilting his head from side to side. "Besides, kids is kids." He stopped and smiled back at Jackson. "If you was a better neighbor, I'd turn you on to a body shop guy who works for cheap. But you ain't. Don't bother me no more. Or I'll call the cops. I'll get a restraining order against you and the old lady for harassment."

***

Jackson and Terri worked on opposite sides of the backyard, each with a rake, each looking down, giving their garden a final cleaning. Neither spoke. Terri went inside and returned with an old bed sheet. They piled in the dead leaves and together tied the corners. They worked against the sun now, under a purple sky, trying to finish before the rain or snow arrived. Jackson lifted the knotted sheet to his shoulder and dumped the leaves at the street for pickup.

Terri was raking behind the camellias when she saw the four newborn kittens, three orange and white and a single black one, huddled in the thick pine straw.

"Look," she called to Jackson.

Jackson stood over the kittens. "You know what this means, don't you?"

"But look at them, Jackson."

"Let's finish up," he said.

They were tying the corners of the last sheet of leaves when Jackson saw the expression on Terri's face. He turned.

The boy, dressed in camouflage, a miniature version of his father, watched from across the yard. Then his unimpassioned eyes slowly lifted to the gathering clouds. A slender serpentine image emerged like an apparition from the shadows behind him. The man carried the rifle low and loose. He stopped, placed a hand on the boy's shoulder, and kneeled beside him. He whispered to the boy, whose vacant eyes remained on the sky.

"Let's go in," Terri said. "I'm tired. We'll finish up tomorrow after work."

"No," Jackson said. He jerked the ends of the sheet into a second knot, then marched toward the man and the boy and sat at the patio table, his back to the neighbors. "Come sit with me," he said.

The man handed the rifle to the boy, turned and headed away, across the far border of his yard. Looking up, the boy began slowly lifting and lowering the heavy rifle, testing its weight. The man disappeared around the corner. As a shadow passed over his thin face, the boy stood alone, hoisting the rifle with the giant scope.

"I'm going inside," Terri said. "Come with me."

"I'm not moving," Jackson said. "This is our yard."

"I don't like it," Terri said.

The boy's hollow eyes turned toward the darkening sky, awaiting a sign.

When the man came back into view, he held an aluminum lawn chair. He leaned forward, unfolding the chair so that it faced Jackson and Terri.

Terri started inside. "Jackson?" she called. He didn't answer. She walked softly, listening for Jackson to follow, then stopped and turned. The boy was down on one knee cradling the rifle, his father standing behind him, whispering. The boy slowly lowered the barrel, resting it on the back of the chair.

"Jackson," Terri called, her voice thin, almost airless.

The boy had one eye near the scope, his hand reaching for the trigger, the barrel still pointed up at a sharp angle. The father's hand rested on the boy's shoulder.

"Jackson!" Terri sprang toward him now, not looking at the boy, only at her husband. She heard the shot. The female Red-tail plummeted from the tall pecan tree, its wings tucked in close. Its body made a soft thud when it struck the ground. The man reached for the rifle, then took the boy's arm and lifted him to his feet. The two turned and walked into their house.

***

"You'll have to make your own lunch," Jackson said to the empty kitchen. "Where the hell are your keys? I'm late. Getting your car to the shop is gonna cost me on the clock." Terri didn't answer. She sat in front of her mirror. "It has to be the thermostat," he said on his way out, "to heat up like that in this weather."

It was their first dark morning, the heavy clouds making it feel more like February than December. The back door banged shut, and Terri heard her husband's footsteps on the walk outside their bedroom window.

Jackson pulled the car door open, relying on the interior light to find the ignition. He pumped the accelerator once and turned the key. A sound like banging fists rattled from under the hood, and for a moment the car shook, then idled. Jackson shut off the engine and pulled the hood latch. At the front of the car, he saw blood spatters on the cement under the passenger door. The bleeding orange and white mother cat, its two front legs broken by the radiator fan, hunched like a fat bunny and drifted from side to side like a drunk. Jackson looked back into the dark garage.

When he stepped out with an axe, Terri was standing over the kneeling cat.

"You might not want to see this," he said. His wife looked down at the cat and tilted her head to the side. She took a step back, looked over at Jackson, then beyond him to the neighbors' house. She crossed her arms over her chest and stared up at him. She waited.

Jackson raised the axe slowly, taking careful aim. As he extended his arms, the muscles in his back contracted. He felt the concussion in his thighs. Terri turned without speaking and marched back inside. He leaned the axe against the wall of the garage where he'd found it, turned and stepped back into the dark dawn of the wet, icy cold morning. He lifted the dead cat by its tail. Before he got to the street, he heard his wife call to him.

"Here," Terri said. She held open an old pillowcase for him. He dropped the bloody cat inside.

They exchanged a look.

"Get my coat," she ordered.

When he returned, the pillowcase was writhing like a bag of angry snakes. He handed her the coat.

"Did you get all four of them?" he asked. She didn't answer. Jackson's eyes turned to the neighbor's house where the heavy, muddy hunting boots stood outside the door. She was knotting the pillowcase. He put his hand over Terri's. "Wait," he said, then crossed the yard.

"Give me the keys," Terri said when he returned, handing him the churning bag. He held the boots in the other hand.

As she backed out of the drive, Jackson set the bloody, squirming pillowcase onto the floorboard between his legs. He dropped in the two steel-toed boots. And as Terri turned onto Cashua Street in the direction of Black Creek, Jackson tied the bag into a knot, exchanged a look with his wife, then tied a second knot on top.

Stevie Baker's Secret Sauce

On the day that Stevie Baker murdered his boss, Marvin Watson, owner of Happy Video, he woke at six a.m. with a bleeding tongue. But that fact is known only to Stevie, and he ain't talking. Stevie is mum. Stevie's taking the fifth. He's your remote on permanent mute.

Stevie's clock was set for nine, which is when he usually woke for work. But the clock was a cheap one that ran on two double-A batteries, the kind that power the bunny in the commercials that run during the Christmas holidays when Stevie felt most depressed about his sister. So distraught was Stevie that the sight of any bunny, even the dead ones on Cashua Ferry Road, reminded him of his sister's one dimple and the cheap diary she kept full of their secrets. But only Stevie knows this. Stevie and his sister, of course.

That morning, bleeding Stevie awakened slowly, not as he usually did—with John Boy and Billy screeching like chimps from the cheap Wal-Mart clock radio with its red nine-zero-zero LED, the piece of crap clock made in China that had been given him by his sister as a Christmas present. She'd wrapped the clock in used red-and-white Santa Claus paper from the year before, paper that had covered the elk-bone-handled hunting knife that Stevie would share with Marvin Watson later in the day.

The wrapping paper had been fine for the knife, but there wasn't enough of it to completely cover the clock radio, which had been assembled, Stevie thought, by a small Chinese fellow with one roving eye on the very day the man suffered a fatal heart attack. His heart failure had been highly unexpected, Steve figured, since the rate of cardiac arrest is much lower in China than it is here, where nobody is much surprised when a guy who assembles clocks, if there is such a guy in America, collapses with a dull thud as Marvin and the Chinaman had. Sometimes Stevie's imagination runs away from him, runs erratically, like a mechanical toy winding down, you know, in that lurching and teetering way, the way Marvin had.

Sitting on their parents' sofa ten feet from the Christmas tree, Silent Stevie listened to the bunny battery commercial on TV as he studied the gift from his sister. Stevie knew that this omission, this incomplete wrapping of the cheap Chinese clock, was code, a time-is-running-out message from his sister, who wouldn't so much as look at him as he ripped Santa's belly the way he would Marvin's later.

Stevie is certain the imaginary Chinaman was as surprised to discover he was dying as Marvin had been. Their surprise may have been identical: that moment of realization. But surely the moments leading up were different, radically different. "Radical" is one of Stevie's favorite words. Somebody shopping in the horror section of Happy Video holds up a DVD and says, "Is this any good?" And if it is, Stevie, standing behind the counter, squeezes his penis real tight, right there at the register where you pay the DVD rental fee, unless you have a coupon for a free one. Stevie nearly chokes his member if the DVD is a Stephen King movie, a really good one like The Shining, until his penis, if anyone could see it, is the color of a radish, and Stevie shouts, "Radical!"

Sometimes when Stevie and his sister shared a special moment, not like the one the Chinaman experienced, but really special, Stevie would ask her what she thought, and she'd turn her head so that her one dimple caught the light just right, and say, "Radical. That was really radical, Stevie," which was also code and peripherally related to his half-dressed Christmas present.

Stevie thinks: There was probably no autopsy performed on the Chinaman. He was dead and the Chinese knew it; and according to The History Channel, although the Chinese have as much capacity to love as anybody, their people often look to the past as a reminder of greatness and happiness, so maybe they find it easier to live with memory than Stevie does. For Mute Stevie there are things he wished he could forget.

Although he isn't saying so, one thing Stevie feels pretty confident about is that the Chinaman didn't die from eating too much pork—even though, again according to The History Channel, few Chinese are Jews and often do eat pork despite the fact that in China pork is not so plentiful as it is in America. There are four Chinese restaurants within a ten-minute drive of Stevie's trailer, one just across the strip mall from Happy Video. And Stevie has learned that what keeps Chinese tickers ticking like an old-fashioned clock is that the Chinese eat lots of vegetables, including cabbage that goes into egg rolls, which are Stevie's favorite but were forbidden him on Saturdays and Sundays by his boss, Marvin, because the cabbage egg rolls produced the most god-awful gas as they worked their way through Stevie's innards. As a result, Chinese cabbage was bad for Happy Video's business, as it was in the end for Marvin himself. Stevie and Marvin Watson, the owner of Happy Video, didn't see eye-to-eye on many things, including Stevie's eating egg rolls on the weekend and Marvin's dating Stevie's sister, Destiny.

Stevie is confident that the Chinaman never ate pork at the Pig Palace, which is right off I-95 at exit 95. It's a long way from China to exit 95. But the Palace is Stevie's favorite place because the ribs are so tender the thick, juicy meat practically melts off the bone. Exit 95 on I-95 is Smithfield, North Carolina, the nearest town to Brogden, or what used to be called Grab Town, where the actress Ava Gardner grew up. Stevie is certain of this. He feels a deep kinship with the dead actress. Her life was both wonderful and tragic, for she never found true love as Stevie had. But for all her tragedy, Ava knew what good Bar-B-Q was—Eastern North Carolina Bar-B-Q, the kind you get at exit 95.

Another thing Stevie knew was that when Ava was married to Frank Sinatra, the two fated but tragic lovers living apart, she in Spain and he in Vegas—this at a time when they were both screwing their brains out but not with each other, that kind of tragic love—in the middle of all that heartbreak, Ava would place a transatlantic takeout order to Scott's Bar-B-Q in Goldsboro, North Carolina, about fifteen miles east of Smithfield, and Howard Hughes would see to it that one of his planes delivered the Bar-B-Q to the lonely Miss Gardner.

Bar-B-Q is a big part of life for many eastern North Carolinians, so it would be of no significance to the court that Stevie was at the Pig Palace the night before Marvin Watson, the pig, got stuck like one. Tight-lipped Stevie used to order the combination plate. It included chopped Bar-B-Q, the only kind there is, a Bar-B-Q chicken quarter, French fries, coleslaw, and hush puppies. You wouldn't know it if you're not from that part of the country, but often the measure of a great Bar-B-Q restaurant is its coleslaw. First it should be cold. (Stevie knows that may sound obvious but challenges you to write in your diary of dirty little secrets every time you do or do not receive coleslaw that is really cold. Your findings would be illuminating and provide pleasant conversation to share with family or friends after church at your favorite Bar-B-Q restaurant.) Next is the mayonnaise factor. Not only should the cabbage be finely chopped and crispy cold but the mayonnaise should not overpower the taste of the cabbage. Although Stevie often produced eye-watering vapors after eating a combination plate at the Pig Palace, he wrote it off to the vinegar and crushed red pepper Bar-B-Q sauce, not the coleslaw.

Stevie didn't order the combination plate anymore because since his sister, Destiny, had stopped going with him to the Palace he had nobody to share his pork with. So now he just ordered the large rib plate, which still came with French fries, coleslaw, and hush puppies.

The thing about Bar-B-Q ribs is that while the meat might be so tender it practically drips from the bone, the pork skin can be as thin and sturdy as the plastic used by the Chinese to ship clock radios. From time to time, a piece of that skin as thin as a razorblade will wedge itself between your back molars, and though you might not even know it when you go to bed at night, while you sleep your tongue will work like the Devil to get that shard out, work so hard it may bloody itself. In your sleep you will feel the discomfort, then the pain, and you may even have dreams about dead bunnies or a Chinaman who builds radios, or like Stevie-With-His-Mouth-Shut, you may have dreams about your sister, irrational dreams that you'd think would disappear as soon as you open your eyes.

But if you wake with the taste of blood in your mouth, as See-No, Hear-No, Speak-No Stevie had, don't be too surprised if you too are overcome by a kind of irrational rage, rage that sticks inside your heart like that razor of pork skin between your teeth. And you can believe Stevie when he says that you, like Voiceless Stevie, will feel the tug of destiny and a stabbing rage. And you will do anything to get it out.

Don Juan's Wanton Love

After packing her suitcase, Sylvia sorted out Leon's daily vitamins and spread them like a winning poker hand on the kitchen counter. She had been leaving Leon for years. But just because she didn't love him anymore didn't mean she wished her husband bad health.

Sylvia's getaway felt more like a memory than a conscious act, and the escape had been so thoroughly rehearsed that her heart and mind were adrift upon a calm sea. As she folded panties and selected shoes for her exodus, her hand was steady, her face content, dreamy. Preparing Leon's vitamins and supplements was Sylvia's way of saying she was already gone and that her leaving was complete and tidy. All she wanted from him now was a clean break, one without tears, one without even a goodbye.

Twisting off the cap to the fish oil supplement, she remembered the pearl earrings in her cut glass jewelry box. Leaving Leon did not include leaving the pearl earrings, which often figured in her post-Leon romantic fantasies. More than once she had toweled dry before her bedroom mirror, then, standing alone and naked in heels, reached for the necklace and the matching earrings. At thirty-two, her flesh soft but assured, her figure harmoniously proportioned, Sylvia saw in the mirror a woman as ripe and ready as a tender fig. As she clasped the necklace, her imagination drifted like a receding tide and her eyes fell into a dreamy repose.

Then from somewhere in the house would echo Leon's voice, and her future with him would unfold before her, the image in the mirror slowly melting like hot wax. "No, no," she would whisper, aghast as her breasts shriveled and sagged, her thighs drooped and thickened. In defiance, Sylvia would press on red lipstick, sending Leon far, far away. "No way," she'd say, her eyes flaming blue as indigo, her revived flesh burning once more with a spirit hot for living.

The earrings. Sylvia paused before entering the musky dim light of the bedroom she shared with Leon. Before her, the brown leather suitcase lay open like a great and wise book. She pictured it resting on the crisp sheets of a North Myrtle Beach motel room, one filled with clean salty ocean air and morning sunshine, one ablaze with life's possibilities.

A quick inventory of the suitcase's contents confirmed a new beginning. But by the time she'd sorted through the neat layers of satin and soft cotton and rearranged her makeup for perfect balance and symmetry, Sylvia had forgotten about the earrings.

"Damn," she said aloud when she re-entered the kitchen and spied the fish oil capsules. Dreaming again of tomorrow, she fetched the earrings then absent-mindedly set them on the counter beside the pills. She didn't want to forget them.

But she did forget them. And around midnight while Sylvia lay dreaming in her oceanfront Rhonda Vu Motel room, Leon came home drunk. He swallowed the pearl earrings along with his vitamins and supplements. Maybe it was something in the metal or in the pearls, or maybe it was the lethal concoction of whiskey, vitamins, and earrings that killed him.

The coroner's report stated only that he died in the shower, that when his heart sputtered he suddenly dropped to a sitting position and just went kaput. His soft, chunky butt made an airtight stopper for the shower drain. And the next morning as Sylvia's neighbor, Trish, stood outside watering her lawn, she looked across the narrow stretch of green cotton that separated her house from Sylvia's and spied water gushing like an open hydrant from beneath Sylvia's house.

Anger and disappointment smoldered inside Sylvia. The life-altering act of leaving Leon, of finally striking out on a new path, had been intended to make a statement loud and clear, but no one heard it. No one even knew she had left him.

Sylvia trudged through the burial arrangements, the funeral and its aftermath, and only she knew that her woe was for herself, not Leon. While he was alive, Sylvia could have left him. But in death Leon had made that clean break impossible. Her husband's sudden departure seemed to Sylvia the ultimate act of fraud and infidelity. In death he had turned the tables on her in true Leon fashion, carelessly. From the hereafter he had fettered her and affixed himself to her spirit like a suckerfish, leaching the life from her. Instead of a widow's emptiness, Sylvia burned with a nervous anticipatory energy, a detached restlessness for the life she had planned. For months everyone, including her neighbor Trish, mistook her highly charged but directionless urgency for grief.

How do you leave a dead man? Sylvia asked herself.

***

It was the Fourth of July holiday, and Trish and Sylvia were having a cold beer beside the Bar-B-Q grill on Trish's deck. Trish, a cosmetologist, wore bright orange Clemson University running shorts. The straps of her black Wonderbra hung from her shoulders like slanted question marks. As they drank, Sylvia stared vacantly into a pyrotechnical sunset while Trish enumerated the blessings of mail order sex aids for young widows. For *vibrator* Trish substituted her euphemism, *boyfriend*.

"Baby," Trish said, resting her hand on Sylvia's thigh, "if you don't unwind, you're gonna have a complex ten feet deep."

"I already got one," Sylvia said, knocking off the last of her Bud Light.

"What?" Trish said. "A boyfriend?"

"No—I mean, yes. What I mean, Trish," Sylvia said, "is that I already have a complex. Mine's six feet deep."

"You got to quit blaming yourself about Leon. He was just a fluke."

"That's true."

"His dying, I mean."

Sylvia reached into her mini-cooler for a cold one. "I'm selling the house and all that's in it, leaving Darlington forever," she said.

"You're only exacerbating the problem if you just up and take off. You can run but you can't hide from it." Trish had majored in Psychology the only semester she attended Horry-Georgetown Technical College, where she had learned, and now liked to flaunt, her one big word.

"I began exacerbating at an early age," said Sylvia.

Trish lifted her beer can before her like a crystal ball, squeezed her eyes half shut like an actress on the soaps, and gazed out past the horizon. Then, slowly and deliberately, she popped the top of a fifth beer while applying her penetrating psychological powers to Sylvia's situation.

"I can read your mind," Trish said with a theatrical nod. "You are highly conflicted."

"How can you read my mind, Trish, when you can't even read my lips? I'm getting the hell out of Dodge."

"You're pent up."

"Thanks," Sylvia said. "You're the answer to all my problems. How much do you charge by the hour?"

Assuming the professional posture of a trained therapist, Trish brought her index fingers together at her lips and pressed in her elbows so that her breasts bubbled in a wondrous way. Her eyes scanned the heavens for wisdom. She released a heavy breath. "I'll admit I'm bi-curious; most women are. But I don't think it would be right between us, and I'd never do it for money. It would be bad for my self-esteem."

"I mean for this shrink session, Doctor. Do you take MasterCharge?"

"See what I mean? That's your subconscious coming out. Those words Master and Charge? You seek domination. That's what you want," she said, nodding emphatically like a frenzied bobble head, then taking a long pull on her beer.

"What I want is to remove myself from the premises."

Trish contemplated as she drank. Then she drank as she contemplated. "Women these days," she said, "they are taking ahold of their sexual freedom, and like there is no turning around now? Boyfriend? Uh-huh."

Sylvia waited. Then slowly tilted her head to one side, like a puppy will.

Trish's bobble became a wobble.

"Let's have another beer," Sylvia said.

"Okay," Trish said.

***

His name was Don Wayne, and he was a natural, an amalgamation of enigmatic, seemingly contradictory features that excited women like a primal subliminal scent. His deep serenity produced a spicy seasoning of mystery that accentuated his dark, brooding good looks. But his powers and abilities, Don knew, were not of his own making, and thus it was his nature to feel a little surprised when a new woman looked at him in that way that made conversation easy, often unnecessary. His lovers sensed a sultry, calm shyness in him, his gratitude and ease on romance's field of play. And for him, every new encounter was a gift.

Unlike his fire fighting co-workers, whose repertoire, outside of fire, was limited to sex and drinking, Don never boasted of his successes, and in his silence lay the kindling of legend and myth. More than once a woman had sent him a drink or separated him from a conversation with another fireman at The Paradise Lounge. So at the station when longwinded, explicit talk about sexual variation or conquest reached the point where validation was required, every face turned to Don. He'd bend his eyes to the floor with that tightlipped uncomfortable smile and mutter something like, "Mostly what you all like to do is talk about it." Then somebody would say, "You're right about that, Don Juan."

When Jody James or Eddie Glad or another fireman found Don alone, he'd ask with wide-eyed sincerity, "How do you do it?"

Don would laugh in that shy way and say, "When God made a woman, he made a fool out of me." Or if they were drunk he'd say something vulgar, in the spirit of the moment, something like, "Well, if it's wrinkled and it wiggles—." But those were just lines intended to sever further discussion. In truth, Don didn't know how to answer. He just knew that he adored women and that women could somehow see or feel that veneration. He loved everything about them, the way their minds worked, especially if they were smart and funny, the way they smelled, his hands upon them, their hands on him. Through a kind of telepathy expressed in subtle gesture and wordless poetry, they communicated to him their deepest needs, their hidden, tempestuous desires.

Don Juan responded in kind, his eyes and body saying, My greatest happiness, my calling, is pleasing you, only you. And in these coded ciphers of sweet lust, he never lied. He was humbled by the bounty that life lay before him, the plentitude of joy that came from his giving. Women were a delicious secret to him. Don knew the act of love was not about putting out a woman's fire. It was about patiently stirring those embers into a tight blue-white pearl of flame and sustaining the heat until a transcendent bliss filled her with rhapsodic euphoria. Making love was not something you talked about; it was something you did because you were wired to do it. Making love was about being present when it happened.

Some men were wired with the uncanny ability to smell fire when others couldn't, but they weren't vain about that ability. Other men were wired with the uncanny ability to start fires, and Don in his shy way saw no reason to feel anything other than grateful for that calling.

***

While economists around the globe scratched their heads and pondered the cause of worldwide economic collapse, Sylvia could answer the question in one word: Leon. The year before Leon's death and without her knowing it, he had refinanced a subprime mortgage to buy a pontoon boat that he lost in a poker game before he ever got the boat wet. Now there were no home buyers, no hint of any. Green fungus obscured the For Sale sign in her front yard. Sylvia couldn't weather the consequences of foreclosure and she couldn't sell. And she couldn't stay.

From some other dimension Leon exerted his spite upon her, condemning her to the confines of the sorry life they still shared. At her dressing table in the morning, she'd glimpse him in her mirror. After midnight, she'd hear him stumble in drunk. In a feeble attempt to even the score, she had given away the bed, replacing it with a cheap rickety one from the Salvation Army. The dining room had become her bedroom, the bedroom a kind of dark forbidden storage crypt for relics of her former life. But eliminating vestiges of Leon did nothing to stymie his omnipresent will. Leon inhabited the place, and he made it known to Sylvia that he was staying put.

Then Leon began following her, appearing at McGoo's Optometry where Sylvia worked as a receptionist. She saw his vague figure, his ghostly form, standing in the endless line of patients shuffling toward blindness, and though her eyes were clear, she felt herself among the legion, the years ahead fading finally into darkness.

Over time, her longing for freedom simmered into a lust for revenge.

***

The answering machine picked up at Trish's shop, Beauty World and Spa, and the recorded voice said, "Hair, nails, and pretty tails." Before Sylvia could leave a message, Trish picked up.

"Sounds like a winner," Trish said. "I been huffin' perm all afternoon. A few cold ones sounds like the ticket."

There was a hint of violence in all of Sylvia's pre-going-out preparations. In the shower, she scrubbed until her loins were bright pink. When she shampooed, her nails raked furrows in her scalp. She toweled dry with a force sufficient for scrubbing scorched pans. Naked, she charged from the bathroom to her closet where she jerked hangers this way and that with an action you might associate with wringing a chicken's neck until she located a dress she'd never worn because Leon insisted it was too short at the bottom and too low at the top. Sylvia flung the dress onto her bed. She hooked her bra like a football player strapping on shoulder pads, and yanked on her black leather boots the way a combat soldier might.

Holding up a tube of lipstick like a blasting cap, she looked contentiously into the mirror. "I dare you," she snarled. Sylvia tilted forward so that she could see down the front of her dress. "Get an eyeful," she said. Then she lifted her skirt until her sexiest panties showed. "Then go to hell." She applied the red lipstick and checked the mirror. Her smile looked like a smear.

***

Inside The Paradise Lounge, Jody James and Eddie Glad had assumed what Don called "the horny cowboy pose." At a twenty-degree angle each rested an elbow against the bar, raised one knee and balanced his boot upon the brass rail near the floor. Like dual high beams, the roving eyes of the firemen raced over every inch of female flesh searching for a spark.

The two could pass as bookends except for their T-shirts. The words across Jody's said, I'm A Member Of The Missile Class and boasted a National Rifle Association patch above his heart. Eddie's shirt featured a cartoon in the fashion of hillbilly humor: In the center of the cartoon "Dixie," a replica of the orange Confederate race car from The Dukes of Hazzard, has smashed into a tree. A crown of stars circles the head of the dizzy, chinless bootlegger staggering from the wreckage. The mangy hound beside him has eyes like fried eggs and ears that stand out like he's being electrocuted. The scrawled words in the bubble above the mountain man's head say, Gee, Spot! My Dixie Wrecked!!

When Don entered the lounge both men lifted their beers in one synchronous movement, and George Miles, who was tending, had a cold one waiting for him. The three firemen touched glasses, drank, and then turned to the crowd, eager for what the night might bring.

***

Trish had opened a second Bud Light when her doorbell chimed. Setting down the beer, she glanced into a mirror. Her hair looked like a freeze-dried soufflé, her makeup a little showy. Across her way-too-tight red T-shirt, the words Taiwan On? stretched wondrously, and the cellophane fit of the short red skirt made her look like a chili pepper.

"Hey," Sylvia said.

Trish's eyes went Betty Davis. "Damn!" she said. "Come on in, darlin'. Whew! You look hot. What'd you do, get you a boyfriend?

Sylvia swung her keys before Trish's eyes like a hypnotist. "You ready?" she said.

"Almost." Trish knocked off the rest of her beer, set the empty can beside the end table lamp, and lifted her own car keys. "I feel like driving," Trish said. "I'm feeling a little wound up." Sylvia gave a questioning nod to the empty beer can. "Okay," Trish said. "You can drive, but we're taking the Mustang. You'll like it. That rumble will remind you of your boyfriend." She winked a big one. Sylvia dropped her keys beside the end table lamp and took Trish's.

Inside the Mustang, Trish grinned and said, "Baby, you look gooood. I like that pearl necklace. You ought to buy you some matching earrings."

"Shut up," Sylvia said.

When the two women stepped from the car outside The Paradise Lounge, they exchanged a conspiratorial nod of camaraderie. "Look," Trish said. "It's a full moon."

Sometimes before sporting events, you watch players become athletes. They leave the locker room as ordinary people, but upon entering the field of competition, a metamorphosis occurs. You can see it, that transformation in physicality. Their bodies become erect with anticipation, a rhythm like the breathing force of life settles upon them, and you behold their ascent. Feeling a slight pang of envy, Sylvia watched as Trish found her stride, her body confident of the promise that lay ahead.

"How long's it been for you?" Trish said. "Since you were in the action?"

"A lifetime," Sylvia said. "Ten years."

Trish draped her arm around Sylvia's shoulder as they walked. "Don't you worry, baby doll. It's like riding a bicycle or a boyfriend. You don't forget. Besides, look at you. You got 'do me' written all over you." She gave Sylvia a little hug. "Ten bucks says you won't be leaving here with me."

By the time Trish reached for the door of The Paradise Lounge, she was no longer Trish; she was the figment of her own imagination, the answer to her own dreams. She held the door and smiled at Sylvia. "Fasten your seatbelt, sister."

***

Shimmering neon beer signs, one blue the other red, commanded the walls at opposite ends of the bar, and in the very middle between the two, in a smoky aura of violet light, stood a tall dark man wearing a pressed white button-down, snug black jeans and cowboy boots—his sapphire blue eyes looking into Sylvia's. The effect upon her was instantaneous and potent. She turned her eyes from his, her fingers levitating to the pearl necklace. Suddenly the music and laughter, the pleasant aromatic blend of beer, perfume and cologne, the smiling faces in the blue and red glow all conspired to assault her senses. Atmospheric pheromone clouds wrenched her breath like dense smoke, while the smoldering source of this rushing and radiant surge of romantic readiness stood alone in a purple shaft of light looking only at her. Trish's voice broke the spell.

"Rule number one," announced Trish doing that inconspicuous up-periscope search of the horizon that is anything but. "Don't let him buy you a drink if you don't want to talk him."

Sylvia wanted to say, I may have lost my stride, but I haven't lost my mind. What she said was, "We'll take turns buying rounds."

"Good idea. I'll buy the first one. Pick you out a man while I'm gone," Trish said. She turned, then stopped and leaned closer. "Hell, pick you out two or three. Girl, you got some catching up to do."

When Sylvia glanced back at the bar, the human landscape shifted. The man in the magic light vanished. "I'll get us a booth if I can find one," she said.

"Girlfriend," Trish said. "If you want some action, you've got to be where the action's at. Besides, those Naugahyde booths? I'd lose a layer of heinie skin."

"You aren't wearing panties, are you?"

"Rule number two. Abandon all non-essentials," Trish said, surveying the jubilant pageant before them. Suddenly, eyes wide, she whirled around in front of Sylvia. "Over my left shoulder," she whispered, "the gorgeous one at the bar. I think he's looking at me."

Sylvia glanced up. Don tilted his head a degree and gave her a slight smile, one that said, I'm glad you're finally here; I've been waiting for you all night. "Who is he?" Sylvia murmured. "What's his name?"

"Who cares what his name is," Trish said. "What you're looking at is one hunka-hunka burning love. I'll be right back."

Trish glided through the crowd toward the bar, giving her walk a little extra oomph, winking or smiling at every man in her league. Sylvia fingered her purse for the cigarettes she'd stopped smoking five years ago. Adrenaline filled her like wind in a schooner's sails. She could hardly breathe, experiencing again that tilt-a-whirl feeling: insides spinning this way and that, raucous oscillating music all around her, bright colors and laughter colliding in a blur. She pressed her palm against her heart and stepped back into a shadow. Although the earth still swayed beneath her, Sylvia felt the return of her balance as the bright carnival settled before her eyes. Swirling currents of laughter surfaced here and there, and a tide of warm bodies swayed with the jukebox.

Somebody bought Trish a shooter at the bar. Sylvia watched as she tossed it back.

Then beside her, a man said, "I thought I knew the name of every pretty flower in Darlington County." Sylvia turned. The patch on his T-Shirt said The National Rifle Association. "But I don't think I know yours." He smiled and took her hand. Sylvia cast about for reinforcements. At the bar, Trish threw back a second shooter. "My guess," he said, "is Rose. Beautiful to look at but dangerous to touch." He bowed slightly. "Name's Jody James."

"Hey," Sylvia said, crabbing her fingers in the bottom of the purse for phantom cigarettes.

"Was I right?" Jody asked. "Rose?"

She was sure the cigarettes were in there someplace. "Sorry," she said, giving up the search. "I'm Sylvia."

"Happy to meet you." The two stood like sentries guarding the crowd. "I put out fires," said Jody.

"What?" She didn't look at him.

"I'm a fireman. You got a fire, I'm your man."

"Nice to meet you," Sylvia said. Now they were two strangers waiting for an elevator. She spotted Trish, swaying like a graceful roller-skater through the commingled bodies.

Jody James said, "Well, Miss Sylvia, can I buy you a drink?"

"Thank you," she said, "but I got one coming."

Without breaking stride, Trish handed her a beer, took her arm, and did a one-eighty. "Come on," she said, "I want you to see something." Trish held her hand as they negotiated the tightly packed bodies. Sylvia's breast nuzzled a muscled shoulder, and strong, warm fingers brushed the slope of her back, light as an ocean breeze. The radiant human heat was intoxicating.

"Hey, darlin'!" Trish called to someone, and when she passed another man she said, "Hey, Les. Did you not know I was here, or are you just playing hard to get?" Les smiled. When they passed, Trish gave his small behind a little pat. As they approached the bar, George Miles, the bartender, smiled and held up two shooters. The blue-eyed man had disappeared.

"You got to see this," Trish said. "This is like the funniest shit I've ever seen."

"There you are!" a man called to Trish. "I thought I'd lost you!" The man was wearing a T-shirt with a hillbilly cartoon on the front.

"Wait," Trish said. She took one of the shooters and handed the other small glass to Sylvia. "Goodbye history, hello now," she said. They drank.

"Hey, I'm Eddie Glad," the man in the T-shirt said. "And I'm glad to meet you."

"Chase it with your beer," Trish said when she saw the look on Sylvia's face. "It tastes just like those speckled candy balls we ate when we were kids—you know, fireballs?" Sylvia lifted her beer. "The drink," Trish said with a big smile. "It's called a fireball." She signaled to George for another round.

"Not for me," Sylvia said.

"I'm Eddie Glad," Eddie persisted. "I'm a fireman. I know all about fire balls."

"What you know about," Trish said, tossing her arm around Eddie's shoulder, "is blue balls."

"It ain't so," Eddie said. "At the station, I'm referred to as 'great balls of fire'."

"You don't know shit about fire," Trish said giving his arm a touch. She was a little drunk.

"Oh no?" Eddie dipped the tip of his finger into his mouth, touched it to Trish's chili pepper behind, then whipped the finger wildly to shake off the imaginary flame. "I know it burns," he said, giving her a little squeeze. Trish pecked Eddie's cheek with a kiss.

Sylvia saw Don Juan, the back of him, leaning over the jukebox. His thighs were thick, his form tightly sculpted. Illuminated from below, his face slowly turned, and the line of his soft brow, high angular cheek, and rugged jaw fell into high relief. His eyes met hers.

Trish pulled Sylvia's arm with a jolt. "Eddie! Eddie!" she shouted. Then to Sylvia, "You've got to see this, darlin'. This is the funniest thing I've ever seen. Show her, Eddie. Show her!" Eddie turned and puffed his chest. Trish burst into laughter and Eddie joined her.

"What?" Sylvia said. Bending, bobbing, clutching their stomachs, the two were red-faced. "What?" Sylvia said. She looked over at the jukebox. No Don.

Collapsing in laughter, Trish took Sylvia's hand. "Read it," she said, pointing at the front of Eddie's shirt.

Sylvia did. "Okay," she said. Her eyes flashed around the room. Trish was laughing again.

"You got to read it," Trish shouted. "You know read it." Sylvia gave her a look. "Out loud!"

"Gee. Spot." Sylvia said the words like a kindergarten teacher to a class of three-year-olds. "My. Dixie. Wrecked."

Trish was pounding the bar like a referee at the end of a wrestling match. "Again!" Trish shouted. "Again!" People turned and stared.

"Gee, Spot. My Dixie wrecked. Gee spot. My Dixie wrecked." Then she heard what she was saying. Her face flushed. She dropped her eyes and patted the pearl necklace. The place was roaring with convulsive laughter. Sylvia turned to the bar, trying as best she could to bend her lips into a smile. She lifted her beer and finished it. When she set down her bottle, George Miles swept it away and set down a cold one in front of her.

"On the house," he said, giving her hand a friendly pat. "You're a good sport."

Sylvia felt Trish's grip on her wrist but refused to turn. Then the hand went limp and fluttered against Sylvia's. "Daaaamn," Trish whispered, swaying to find her balance. Sylvia glimpsed a man over her shoulder.

Trish swooned, "I got three things to tell you, Eddie." She couldn't take her eyes from Don. "Daaaamn," she said again. Then she swung her face toward Eddie. "I forgot the other two."

Eddie said, "Where you been, Don? You missed it, man, you missed it."

Don nodded in the direction of the jukebox. Then he looked at Sylvia. Vince Gill's If You Ever Have Forever In Mind began. He offered his hand. Sylvia took it.

The tiny dance floor was steamy and crowded, but when Don took her into his arms, Sylvia's eyes faded and she floated weightlessly upon a soft sea, the heat of the summer sun bathing her face. His hands were strong and tender, his chest hard and tender, his breathing soft and tender. He didn't speak and neither did she.

The song was over, but Sylvia hadn't heard it end. Only when his hand touched her hair did she awaken. As she turned and started back to the bar, his fingers stroked the small of her back as if she were still that sleek schooner and he the pilot at the helm. They sat in the soft red light at the end of the bar.

Time passed into no time. They talked or didn't. A song began and Sylvia turned to watch without seeing the couples on the dance floor. She felt his fingertips upon the inside of her arm, a touch so light it could have been his breath upon her hand or face or back, and in that touch he said, Please don't go.

At some moment in this evening without time, Trish's voice caught Sylvia's attention. "Sylv-ya?" In Trisha's rendition the name had one syllable, not two. Trish stood on the deck of a rolling ship. "Sylvia? I wan' you to meet somebody. Sylvia? This is Les? Les, Sylvia? Sylvia? Les is more. Get it? Les is more." She turned to Les and grasped his shoulder with both hands to steady herself. "I got to show you something," she announced to him. "This's-like-the-funnies'-thing-I've-ever-seen. You've got to read it." She and Les disappeared.

Sylvia and Don lifted their beers. Don said, "Do you believe that, 'Less is more'? The expression, I mean."

"No," Sylvia said, "I believe less is less."

"Is that always bad?"

"With the exception of perfume, I'd say so."

"Is that why you're not wearing any?"

Sylvia suddenly realized the omission and how long she'd been out of the game. She looked up at him. Don touched his finger to his nose.

"You're a fireman, too, huh?"

He smiled. "Less may not be more, but at certain moments less can be better, like the smell of you versus the smell of not you." He smiled again.

A jarring anxiousness swept over Sylvia like a cold ghostly draft. An alarm sounded inside her, followed by an aura of duality that settled over everything. It was the feeling you might associate with certain dreams, when you're aware that you're dreaming; the haunting feeling of being both participant and observer of uncontrollable events as they unfold. Suddenly, everything meant something else.

"You would think that the bigger the fire, the more water it'd take to put it out," Don said. But that's not always true." This was code, Sylvia was sure. And she knew the translation, and in the translation she felt exposed, transparent, defenseless. "Take this example," Don said. "Back when people around here raised more cotton, they'd pack closed train cars for shipment to market." Sylvia remembered Trish's lecture on Freud and the meaning of trains. "The boxcars would be so tightly packed that forces of nature would sometimes take over." Sylvia felt the constriction of her insides, the compression of her breathing. His hand stroked hers. "For as soft and tender as you'd think cotton is, if you pack it too tight, the friction of its fibers can start a fire." Sylvia reached for her beer.

"Those fires," Don said, "they can smolder and burn, sometimes forever." All air emptied from The Paradise Lounge. "For years, there seemed no way to put them out." From some watchtower high above the bar, eyes—hers and someone else's—looked down on her as Don continued. "To get to the source of the fire meant opening the steel boxcar, which fed oxygen to the fire, making it burn even hotter." She couldn't breathe.

"I have to go now," Sylvia gasped. She grabbed her purse and lunged from her barstool.

Near the silent jukebox, Trish and Eddie Glad waltzed to their own music. "You have to read it," Trish was saying. "It has two meanings."

"We have to go, Trish," Sylvia said. "It's late." She glanced back at Don, who sat with his back to her.

"You need readin' lessons, baby doll," Trish slurred.

"I'm Eddie Glad," Eddie reintroduced himself to Sylvia. "I'll be glad to take her home."

She looked around for help. George Miles was collecting bottles and cans from empty tables. "I'll see to it that she gets home safe," he assured Sylvia. "Won't be the first time." He smiled and nodded toward the door.

***

Sylvia sat behind the wheel of Trish's Mustang staring across the narrow moonlit field of green cotton at her own dark house. She couldn't go there. She'd witnessed the abundance of life on the other side, and she just didn't think she could return to the destitute life on this side, the hollow world inside that house. Still hers was a world robbed of choices.

She lifted her chin and trudged from the car. Exhausted and mindless, Sylvia fished inside her purse for a house key. And it was only after she had summoned all her will to open that door that she realized it was staying locked.

There was no house key on the ring. Her keys lay beside Trish's lamp, on the end table. And by now Trish was in La-La Land, God knows where. Sylvia dropped her purse, collapsed onto the steps, and, bending forward, rested her face in her open palms. She didn't cry; she didn't feel like crying. What she felt were the vanishing remains of her life, the dead cinders of body and soul, blown like sand into a dead sea. What she felt was a rising tide of nothingness. Leon had shackled her to a loveless house, forced her to live in it after he was gone, and now he was applying the finishing touches by refusing her access to the very thing she most didn't want.

For a fleeting minute, Sylvia told herself that Trish would appear at any time, that she would sleep over at Trish's, even if it meant a night of holding her friend's head over the toilet. At least she would be free of Leon's otherworldly grip. In the morning, she'd think of something. She didn't know what, but something. She sat and waited. She looked up at the bright moon. Finally she thought she might break a window.

Then she heard Leon's whining voice. You don't have to break a window. I never fixed the one you nagged me about, the one on the side of the house.

"Shut up," she said aloud. Then she remembered Leon's excuse for not replacing the latch. "There might be an emergency," he'd said. "We might get locked out, or there might be a fire."

Fortunately, the window was just above the heating and air conditioning unit. She slipped out of her heels and hoisted herself up. The full moon gave her plenty of light. She pressed her fingers under the window frame, and the weak seal of dirt and gunk gave way. Still the window, a little swollen on one corner, did not go up easily. She jimmied it, taking one corner up an inch or two and then the other, until finally she wedged her head and shoulders into the narrow space.

Because of the brilliant moonlight, the unlit interior was black as a cave, and she blindly extended her arms feeling for a chair. As she stretched forward, her lovely heart-shaped behind nudged the frame.

The window came down like a guillotine. And it would not yield.

So now the most fiendish of reversals. An hour earlier, the feeling of being within and outside of simultaneously had made her flee Don Wayne and The Paradise Lounge. Now that her retreat was complete, she was trapped inside a netherworld where she was neither inside nor out. Instead, she dangled literally between the two. She thought she heard distant laughter. Into the dark room, Sylvia screamed, "I hate you, Leon! I hate this house! I hate you!"

Leon's reply was an emphatic one: The half-opened window had allowed a rush of summer air into the house. The elevation in temperature communicated to the thermostat that the air conditioning should kick on. And when it did, Sylvia felt her dress balloon open like a parachute. Her satin panties glowed like a luminous pearl in the moonlight. Instead of lying awake in some North Myrtle Beach motel room listening to the gentle slap of ocean waves, free of Leon and this hell, she lay in the jaws of the house Leon had built. And that soft slapping sound was the hem of her dress against the window glass.

"I will not cry; I will not cry," Sylvia repeated to herself.

***

Headlights glinted against the dining room wall. "Trish! Trish!" She waited. She listened. She drew in as much air as circumstances permitted. "Trish! Trish! Triiiish!" she shouted again. Still nothing. She called out again. Again, nothing. Sylvia collapsed, limp as a wet rag. There was nothing left but humiliation and surrender. No one could hear her above the churning air conditioner.

A hand touched the inside of her ankle. Hot electricity shot through her loins. "Steady," Don said. His powerful arm circled her hips. His thighs radiated against her bare legs, and when he lifted the window, his fingers brushed her thin panties. He held her with one arm as he pushed the window up. "I'll help you inside."

In the darkness of the room, a shaft of moonlight fell across one side of Sylvia's bed. She and Don sat side by side, silently in the deep shadow. She didn't reach for a lamp. Time became no time. Moonlight slowly peeled away the darkness and uncovered them.

"How do you do it?" Sylvia whispered. "Put out those fires, the ones trapped inside."

"Do you mean in the boxcars, or trapped in other places?"

"Boxcars."

"You identify the hot spot, by spraying the car with water. The area that dries first is the hottest. Then with a giant can opener you cut a small V, not large enough to let in much air. Just enough to get water inside. Only takes about a gallon. It's converted to steam, and that puts out the fire."

"Less is more?" Sylvia said.

"Yes." He reached for her hand, and she let him take it.

"Sometimes," he whispered, "a little thing, a thing as simple as a human touch can start a fire, or put one out."

She pulled her hand away. "It's too late," Sylvia said. She pushed herself from the bed and drifted to the window.

He watched her, the moonlight so bright that he could see the line of her flesh through the thin, short dress. Don said, "You think it's too late." She didn't answer. "But it's not," he said. "Look."

When she turned, Don was holding her car keys. "Go pack your suitcase," he said.

"I'm not going anywhere with you," she said. "I need a vacation."

"Then go pack for one," he said. "Go on."

Sylvia was too exhausted, too dispirited to resist. There was no way she could spend the night in Leon's house. Packing a suitcase suddenly seemed the only thing she could do. She found the brown leather one and began dumping whatever clothes and makeup she could feel in the dark. Don called from another room.

"You got a toolbox?"

"The window?" she said. He didn't answer. "Back porch." She stood before the mirror, holding the suitcase—staring at the dark shadow of herself.

"Where's the electrical panel?" he called.

"What?" she said in a dreamy voice.

"Never mind," he said.

When Sylvia entered the small dark living room, Don was standing at the open front door. "I'm not going to your place," she said.

"No," he said, "you're not. But you are leaving this one." He reached for her leather bag.

Neither of them spoke as they crossed Sylvia's yard under the full light of the summer moon to the driveway of Trish's house, where both their cars were parked. Don opened her trunk and set the suitcase inside. Pressing her keys into her palm, he stepped close enough to kiss her. When she looked up, she saw his blue, blue eyes in the soft moonlight. The roar of cicadas suddenly ceased. More than anything she wanted him to kiss her. But he didn't. She closed her eyes and whispered.

"Could you—"

"Yes," he said. She felt his radiant fingers move up her waist, over her back, onto her neck. She smelled him, the smoky musk of his body. She awaited the kiss. Instead he spoke to her. "Spontaneous fire," he said. "It can come at the speed of light."

Still he didn't kiss her. Looking again into his eyes, she said, "A fire like that, how does it get started?"

He smiled. When he stepped back, she felt the pearls slip from her neck. They glowed in his open palm like beads of light. "Could begin with that curling iron you forgot to turn off," he said looking down at the pearls. Sylvia smiled. He folded his fingers over them. "Or," he said, "could be something unexpected that arcs inside your power box, if you know what I mean." Her eyes didn't look away from his. He dropped the pearls into his shirt pocket.

"I know all about that kind electricity," she whispered.

Don stepped back and opened her car door. "The insurance man will explain when he settles your claim."

At the end of Trish's drive, Sylvia made a right turn and headed east, toward North Myrtle Beach. Don headed west, back to Darlington. When she lowered her window to let the warm night air in, she glanced back to see Don Juan's red taillights disappear.

And then, above the pines separating her from Leon and that house, a sudden geyser of brilliant white light erupted.

Sylvia pressed the gas pedal until she could press it no more, and in her mirror she watched as the flames, like a spontaneous, blissful dance, leapt up and up in a frenzy of wild, emancipated joy, a dance of wanton love.

Speck-no's Beach

Speck-no's K-9 Face

Warren Spector, who had been born with the face of a Rottweiler, acquired the name "Speck-no" in the 90's when he worked as a light & sound technician for a South Carolina Rock band called The Wobblers. The band's name flowed easily from the lips of drunks, and The Wobblers became famous in the Southeast among the fraternity set. You might remember their two minor hits, If You Ain't Here After What I'm Here After, You'll be Here After I'm Gone and We Got Racin' Cars.

As a kid, Speck-no had, like most roadies, dreamed of becoming a performer himself. He'd always harbored the conviction that he was the receptacle for a gift, something to share, something like music. He woke with that feeling and carried it into his dreams at night.

When Warren was in junior high, his parents split up. His dad bought him a set of drums and delivered them to the boy's house, where he lived with his mother. But when Warren commanded his foot to play in quarter notes, his right hand to play in half notes and his left to play in whole notes, the mixed messages produced a look and a sound resembling a seizure. Still he didn't give up.

Warren practiced tirelessly, rising at five in the morning and slogging over to his drum kit before breakfast, then picking up the sticks again in the afternoon as soon as he returned from school. His timing didn't improve, but his strength did. The thud of his bass drum vibrated windows in the basement, and the attack on his snare rattled silverware in the kitchen.

On Christmas Eve, he came home from a movie called That Thing You Do and entered his room to discover his mom sitting in a tight knot on the floor beside his bed surrounded by a crude fort constructed of shattered cymbals, twisted hardware, and busted drumheads, a vodka bottle between her legs.

On the drive home from the rehab hospital, Warren told his mom that he would give up his drums if he could take singing lessons. "I just want to be somebody," he said. The next morning at breakfast, he repeated his quest. "I want to please people," he said. "I want to be a star." Without a word, his mom levitated from her chair like a zombie and slowly dragged a stepstool over to the tall cabinet where she kept the aerosol cleaning supplies. He took her hand before she reached inside. "Mom, I've changed my mind," he said, looking up into her vacuous eyes. She teetered at the top of the stool steps. "I think I'd like to work at the zoo," Warren said. His mom hesitated, as if she were trying to remember an omission from her grocery list, then slowly climbed down.

In the months that followed, Warren spent hours before the mirror watching as his limbs lengthened, while patches of hair and clusters of pimples multiplied. Every day he prayed for a transformational reorganization of his face. But as the months passed, its K-9 qualities became more sharply and unquestionably defined. On the street, young children stopped, stared, and then clawed their way up into their mother's arms.

Still the music inside Warren vibrated like a tuning fork. Maybe, he thought, he would become an actor. Actors didn't necessarily possess handsome faces. Distinctive ones would do, especially if you didn't mind playing supporting roles or the part of Wolfman.

Warren Spector, who had been born with the face of a Rottweiler, took up weight training and electronics in high school, where he was well liked by most kids, despite the slope of his forehead and the length of his jaw. His cheerful persistence made up for a lot. Even some of the better looking girls sometimes sat at the lunch table with him, but even at sixteen girls can smell desperation at a distance equaled only by blowflies and raw meat.

***

Speck-no's Howl

Warren was no quitter. The drama club provided proximity to the best looking women in high school. And in drama class he discovered he did have a talent. He not only had the face of a dog; he could bark like one, too. His fifteen minutes came during the high school state basketball championship, where he charged up and down the sidelines of the court barking the opposing team to distraction. The home crowd cheered him. He became the sixth player on the court.

Overtime. Warren stood under the backboard, fifteen feet from the foul line, facing the opposition's star player. He drew a deep breath. Air ball. Big trophy. And for a few precious seconds, he wore a coat made of cheerleader breasts.

Speck-no soon accepted that as far as women went he'd probably never drink from the top shelf. He didn't care. Just give him someone loveable, he prayed—someone with breasts.

***

How Speck-no Got His Name

Warren saved his money and bought a light system, and soon local and regional bands were requesting his services. After a year, The Wobblers hired him on salary. The band played frat parties and small clubs from Biloxi to Charlottesville. But at the end of the night while each of the Wobblers was groping a groupie, Warren Spector was packing up his gear or eating runny eggs at the Waffle House. Occasionally, after a keg party, Warren would volunteer to drive a semi-conscious coed back to her sorority house. He'd exercise every permissible move to take advantage of the girl's blurred vision. But Warren Spector was no pervert. The closest he'd ever come to a quasi-sexual experience was having a fat sorority pledge go down on her knees and fill his jockey shorts with purple puke. For a while, his expectations were challenged.

The band members began to call him Speck-no Poontang.

Over the next six years, membership in The Wobblers turned over at an accelerating rate. As old members dropped out to find day jobs, new and often better players replaced them. But The Wobblers' fan base was slowly eroding, and by the late nineties, Speck-no was exploring other opportunities.

Every option had its prerequisite though. Access to women. He would not give up. He'd seen too many of them, been too close, dreamed too much. Howled at the moon too often. Having spent nearly a decade on college campuses and in bars, Speck-no had learned that if he avoided booze and drugs he could hide enough dough from Uncle Sam to live like a king. He'd always be in the company of available women. And one day his queen would come.

"There's a reason they call it love," he'd say when The Wobblers teased him. "It's a numbers game, but there's somebody for everybody. Half the population is women," he'd say. "And underneath their clothes, they're all naked. There's one out there somewhere for me."

The Wobblers just lowered their heads, "Speck-no poontang," they'd say. Still, he believed what he said.

***

Speck-no's Bleak Future

After leaving the band, Warren took a job at a Myrtle Beach Disco called Rocket Science. Near the end of the summer, the owner, a guy named CP, called Warren Spector into his office after closing and asked him to sit down.

"I can't believe it, Speck-no," CP said. He was pouring himself a full glass of Jack Daniels. "I didn't think it could be done."

"What's that?" Speck-no said.

CP staggered over to Warren, draped one hand over his shoulder and led him to the open office door.

Sweeping his unsteady arm before him, indicating the bar area, CP said, "Square feet. How many? Best guess."

Speck-no sized it up. "Nine thousand," he said.

"Daaaa-ammmn," CP said. "You're gooood. Nine thousand. That's right. You're right on the money, there, Bo." He wagged his head from side to side. "Speck-no, ole-buddy-ole-pal, I somehow managed to put all nine thousand of those square feet up my nose. I gotta let you go."

Speck-no spent the next two weeks consulting bankers and lawyers, investigating what it would take to open his own nightclub on the Grand Strand. But the price of real estate, the cost of a state liquor license—above and below the table—local corruption, red-haired-stepchildren of real mobsters, and legitimate competition were daunting for a light man from a frat band. Still, night after night, he dreamed of the bikinis, the sheer number of them on the sunny stretch from Cherry Grove to Garden City. Take out the in between, he thought, and you've got Cherry City.

When he stopped by to pick up his last paycheck at Rocket Science, CP was all liquor, cocaine, and tears.

"I'm sorry, Speck-no. I'm gonna miss you, Bo. Nobody could clear out a joint at closing time like you. You were the best, man."

"Look," Speck-no said. "How's 'bout we work out a deal so's I can buy you out. You know, maybe a payment plan."

CP opened a drawer and set his buddy Jack Daniels on his desk. "You don't want this joint," he said. "It's cursed. Besides, you can't make any money in Myrtle Beach clubs anymore. It's not like the old days." He poured himself a drink. "What you ought to do is find a way to take the beach somewhere else, somewhere where people don't have one."

"Like how?" Speck-no said.

"Hell, if I knew the answer to that, I'd be in Fat City, now wouldn't I? You find a way to get the sun, the sand, and the suds someplace other than the beach, and they'll be calling you Speck-some." CP held out his unsteady hand. "Good luck, Bo," he said.

"How's about my check?" Speck-no said.

CP handed him an envelope. Speck-no walked away.

"You may want to hold that a couple of days, just to be sure it'll clear." Speck-no was near the door. "Do it," CP called out. Warren stopped and turned. "Just for old time's sake," he said from behind the desk. "Like you always did, you know, clear 'em out in five minutes. You know, one last time."

Speck-no's bark rattled the barren walls.

"Dammed if you ain't the best, man, the best."

When Warren neared the exit he turned and looked back at CP, who was standing on his desk, head down, holding his flaming cigarette lighter high above his head. "You were the best, man," he repeated.

The next morning, Warren Spector sorted through his credit card bills. On the bottom of the pile was the envelope. Along with the bad check, CP had included a note and a ticket to what old timers still called the Rebel 500 NASCAR race held in Darlington every spring. The note said, "Am expecting IRS visit this weekend. Better for you to be out of town. Will tell them they are barking up the wrong tree."

***

Speck-no's Stroke of Good Fortune

Airplanes fall on some people. Some people win the state lottery. The two events can happen on the same day, under the same sky. On the last day of March, in the stands of the Darlington International Raceway, with accumulating particles of spent black rubber on his face and his eardrums bleeding, Warren Spector felt the first breeze of good fortune.

His ticket placed him in a seat beside two women with hair the color and density of tar. They had come equipped with a cache of cold beer. One was named Dirk, the other Tasha. Dirk was a nurse anesthetist, Tasha, a college English professor. The two wore identical Harley tank tops and assorted tattoos. Both had breasts. Neither wore a bra.

At lap three hundred, a black cloud and a crackle of lightning triggered a sudden and violent shower that drenched the fans and stopped the race. The temperature fell ten degrees. Fifty thousand nipples stood at attention. The four standing beside Speck-no were the most perfect he'd ever seen. He heard the voices of angels.

Dirk and Tasha gave him a courtesy smile and reached for another tall Bud. While the cars were in the pits, the two women began making bets. Unaware that their earplugs were in, they, like surrounding fans, spoke at 150 decibels.

"ASK HIM!" Dirk screamed, grabbing Speck-no by his thick muscled forearm and pulling him toward her. Dirk pointed at Warren

Spector's arms. "NICE!" she said, her head bobbing a little. She looked back at her friend. "ASK HIM!" she repeated.

"WHADDA THINK DIRK HERE CAN BENCH PRESS!?" Tasha shouted. "GIVE IT YOUR BEST SHOT." Dirk stood, lifted her arms, curled her wrists, and thrust her chest forward. Another inch and Speck-no might have lost an eye. He took a breath. He looked her over, and over, and over.

"Two sixty-five," he answered.

"WHAD HE SAY!?" Tasha said.

"WHAD HE SAY!?" Dirk said.

Speck-no repeated himself.

"SEEEEE!" Dirk said, "I TOL-JA!!" When she smiled, he tried not to look at her teeth. She ran her hand up his thigh and gave it a squeeze; his left testicle did a summersault. She offered him a beer, and he took it.

By lap 400, Tasha and Dirk, who stood at attention each time Dale Earnhardt, Jr. roared by, tilted back their heads, and did wolf calls in unpredictable, dissonant harmonies. Speck-no opened another beer. He rose from his seat, drew in a deep breath, and let loose a howl. Hundreds of faces turned like score cards at the Olympics. Dirk and Tasha looked at him, then looked at each other. "DAAAAAMMMMN," they said.

When the checkered flag came down, Warren stood between the two women, an arm around each. The three held hands as they left the track area. "WHERE ARE YOU PARKED!?" Tasha asked. The crowd was thick as gnats.

"Somewhere over there," Speck-no said, pointing beyond the mass.

"WHAD HE SAY!?" Tasha asked.

"WE GOT US A MAJOR MALFUNCTION JUNCTION HERE," Dirk said. "HOW'S BOUT A LITTLE TAILGATE PARTY TILL THINGS CLEAR OUT?"

Speck-no climbed on the back of Dirk's Harley, resting his arms around her thick midriff, feeling the unfamiliar sensation of his body against hers. Tasha trailed as they threaded the traffic. Warren closed his eyes and whispered a thank you for every turn, every bump. The two cycles took Pinedale, a small two-lane country road to a stop sign, made a right onto Billy Farrow Highway, and within ten minutes were in the center of Darlington, which remained undisturbed by the pandemonium surrounding the small town. Tasha turned off Main Street between a railroad track and an old, vacant tobacco warehouse the size of a football field. Around back, they powered their bikes up a ramp. Tasha forced the wide dock door open, and they parked the Harleys inside.

"Look at the size of this place," Speck-no said. "Forty-five thousand square feet."

By the time they had dismounted, the rain was coming down in gray sheets. When Tasha and Dirk removed their earplugs they heard the hard rain. They looked at one another, wide-eyed.

"Daaaaammmmmn," they said in unison.

The three sat on the loading dock at the rear of the giant warehouse watching the night come down through the rain. They ate Bar-B-Q sandwiches and drank beer. Speck-no listened as Dirk and Tasha exchanged Dale Earnhardt stories. A few hours later, after a long, reverent pause, Dirk said, "Hell, we're out of beer. Road trip!" When she tried to stand, the earth slipped from under her.

"I'll get these," Warren said. "Where's the nearest place?"

"SAV-WAY's 'bout four blocks," Tasha said, her arm floating before her. "If you go out that way," she said, motioning toward the opposite end of the warehouse, "you'll stay out of the rain."

Speck-no counted his steps, one hundred thirty paces. More than 45,000 square feet, he thought.

Through the dirty windows at the far end of the building, he saw dim streetlights. He unlocked the door and stepped outside. The rain had stopped, but a thin mist soaked the cool spring air. He walked past the SAV-WAY to the town square, past Jewel's Lunch Box, down past the old Coggeshall's Building, to the Once Again consignment shop. He crossed the street and read the inscription on the monument for the Darlington County Confederate dead, then turned and bought beer on the way back.

Back inside the cavernous warehouse, he again counted his steps in the darkness. Ahead, framed by the open dock door, Speck-no saw that Dirk and Tasha had spread two sleeping bags. On one of the bags, the two lay arm-in-arm, asleep.

***

Speck-No's Sudden Intuitive Realization

Defeat has many smells. Some varieties have the odor of dirt and sweat, some the fragrance of last night's perfume, others the stink of a broken dream. But as Speck-no crossed the bridge at Gallivant's Ferry, the halfway point back to Myrtle Beach, he thought that the smell of rain and warm beer and Harley leather held something like a promise. He looked down at the two Polaroid photos beside him on the front seat of his truck. In the first, he and Tasha struck a chummy pose, one arm over the other's shoulder like two linebackers after a brutal victory. In the second snapshot, he sat snuggled up behind Dirk on her Harley. With one hand, she had pulled down her tank top, exposing a breast. The other hand pointed up at the large sign nailed to the side of the warehouse. It read For Sale.

On any other day, Warren Spector might have considered calling it quits—out of work, no prospects of a future, jealous of one woman's love for another. But today, cruising into Conway, Speck-no felt the warm afterglow that even proximity to female love can leave on a man. If sleeping four feet from two lesbians left him with the taste of warm syrup and a lightness of spirit, he knew that the taste and feel of a woman who preferred men was his destiny. A generalized affection for the world swept over Warren, though he didn't know why.

The words Sun! Surf!! And Suds!!! were still on the sign outside CP's club, but in place of Rocket Science were the words Closed for Remodeling.

As he pulled into the empty lot, Speck-no imagined CP's strategic retreat from the IRS: bar tables piled against the entrances and exits, filing cabinets barricaded against his office door, CP at his desk, abusing his thin septum and fragile liver, resisting to the end.

Two announcements were posted outside the chained front door. One said NOTICE, followed by print so small Speck-no knew the worst had come to CP. An unsteady hand had composed the other message. BEWARE OF THE DOG, it said, and scrawled in smaller letters near the bottom, the words HA-HA.

Despite the bad checks and broken promises, Warren Spector regretted that he'd not made it back from Darlington in time to share his mysterious feeling of good fortune. CP's destination was about as far as you could get from good fortune, he thought.

Speck-no slid the key into his truck's ignition, shifted into reverse, glanced into his rearview mirror at the Sun! Surf!! Suds!!!, then looked down at the Polaroids taken under the giant warehouse For Sale sign. "Fat City," Speck-no whispered.

And in that one blinding moment, Warren Spector experienced the illumination that comes from a loving God, that singular instant when not only the planets align themselves just so, but when whole galaxies step aside and clear the way to paradise.

***

Speck-no's Bright Idea

Including the dock at the far end of the warehouse, there were fifteen loading bays. For five days, a convoy of dump trucks drove seventy-five miles to highway construction sites at Garden City and Cherry Grove, backed up to front-end loaders, did a sexy little rear-end dance, then returned seventy-five miles and piled their beach sand into the giant warehouse. Standing at the spot where he and Dirk and Tasha had camped, Speck-no looked over the long stretch of dunes that banked against its walls.

The week before, two paint crews had sprayed the ceiling sky blue and stapled parachutes into billowing white clouds. Warren had hung the stereo speakers himself and installed the fans and saltwater-scented aerosol sprayers discreetly. Now he stepped over to one of the control panels mounted near the rear bay door, closed his eyes, and threw the top switch. The sound and smell of the ocean satiated his senses. "Sand and surf," he whispered.

He turned and looked down the length of the building. Pulling a notepad from his hip pocket, he considered the layout and sketched the interior's design. From end to end, a boardwalk lined with living palmetto trees. Between the banked dunes and the boardwalk, facades from the Myrtle Beach strip. In the center, three rectangular bars, thirty feet long, evenly spaced and separated by patio tables and colorful umbrellas. "Suds," he said, closing the notebook, then stuffing it into his pocket. He smiled to himself, a big, wide grin, an acknowledgement of his moment of pure genius, the premonition of his dream come true. He spread his arms wide. "And next," he shouted, "the sun!" Then he exerted a yelp that slammed against the far wall and came back to him like a promise of love.

As if on cue, the eighteen-wheeler Speck-no had been waiting for pulled into the lot. Loaded with tanning beds.

A truth is a truth. And all of us at some time in our life are blessed with the realization of at least one truth, one thing we are so sure of that our confidence cannot be shaken. Warren Spector had been blessed with three, one following directly behind the other: Truth #1) Women will spend money on a tan. Truth #2) Women who spend money on a tan will find ways of displaying the tan they pay for. Truth #3) Women who display their tan while drinking liquor will attract men who will spend enormous sums of money to watch women drink liquor as they display their tans. Suntans are to women what cars are to men, Warren realized. And at the crossroads of nearly naked women and liquor you will find men with money to pay for the privilege of watching the traffic.

The tanning bed profits would supply the sun and pay the mortgage. Operating expenses would be covered by the sale of tanning supplies, sunglasses, and skimpy swimwear. Add to these monthly rental fees for lockers and showers. The suds would be all profit. It was a beautiful plan.

As the last of the tanning beds was unloaded and installed behind the Myrtle Beach façade, Speck-no walked to his small office at the end of the building. He circled Labor Day on his desk calendar, and wrote, Speck-Some Beach opens. Darlington's fall race would be held that weekend. Fifty thousand race fans, only three miles from his beach.

The telephone rang, but he'd learned not to answer it. Though the race was two months away, Speck-Some Beach had already attracted investment interests from all across the tobacco belt. Today, one message was an offer from the owner of a NASCAR-theme steak restaurant, Red Meat Rally, proposing a franchise package and supplying a list of investors who had already signed on to back the concept of Speck-Some Beach. The manager of The Wobblers had also left a message, offering the band's services opening night for free. Television crews from four states had shown up over the past month to get the story, but Speck-no was no fool. He would allow no pictures and permit no interviews. Nobody had to tell him about the power of a tease.

Like true love and inspired sex, it had all been so very easy. After Warren had maxed out his first credit card, all fear left him. Twenty cards, twenty thousand-dollar limit on each. And now investors were standing in line with millions, eager to hand over big chunks of that money for access to his dream.

***

Speck-no Sees the Face of Doom

Some people win the state lottery. Airplanes fall on some people. The two events can happen on the same day, under the same sky.

Sitting now behind his desk at Speck-Some Beach, Warren was getting the feeling that a turd the size of Montana had singled him out, hunted him down, and was about to dump on him. That turd had a name. She went by Bull, or that's what she said her friends called her. One minute into the conversation, Speck-no knew she was no friend, and the next minute when he said Bull, he meant bullshit.

"This building is one hundred years old," she said. "That makes it historic. You can't turn an historic building into a tanning bar."

"Bullshit," Speck-no said.

The woman wore bulky coveralls and army boots. When she tilted back her defiant chin, he saw the menace in her eyes.

"You look like a woman who would take a dare," Speck-no said, with as much charm as he could conjure.

"I dare you to kiss my butt," she said.

"I'll take that dare," Speck-no said.

"Shut your nasty mouth. I'm gonna do some crawling around to see what kind of damage you've already done to this site." She had the square jaw of a boxer, the four-legged variety. Her straight black hair was cut like Cleopatra's. "You might want to get busy emptying this place of sand, surf, and suds," she said. Bull turned, pulled a baseball cap from the hip pocket of her oversized coveralls, and headed toward the far end of Speck-Some Beach. Aside from the graceful sway of her bottom, there was nothing in those clothes to even say she was a she.

Speck-no watched as the dream killer passed facades of The Pavilion, The Galleon, The Showhouse, and The Bowery. The sun shone, the parachute clouds softly shifted, the perpetual blue sky hovered above, the sound and smell of ocean waves filled the air, and the three long bars waited in the shade of living palmetto trees. This was it, his version of paradise, his dream palace. He couldn't believe that fate in the form of one Susan S. Odom, Bull, might put its disapproving lips together and blow away the bright flame of his dream with one small puff. He couldn't believe it.

He stood thinking. As Speck-Some Beach had neared completion, Warren's quest evolved into a duty—to show that given the right place and the right time, there was somebody for everybody. His conviction grew to universal proportions. Speck-Some Beach would be that place, he had said, at perpetually the right time. During the final phase of preparation, when the lights had gone up and the music of The Wobblers wobbled from the speakers, Speck-no joined the ranks of the few who answer a calling greater than themselves. All over North and South Carolina and in parts of Virginia and Georgia, women dedicated to preserving and deepening their tan counted the days. All over the South men counted their money. Opening night was less than a week away.

Sitting alone now in his office, Warren thought again of CP, assaulted by forces he couldn't combat, sinister forces out to shut him down and haul him off to a place where the sun never shines.

Bull appeared at his door. "I'm quoting now from the Secretary of the Interior's Standards for Treatment of Historic Properties," she said. Speck-no felt his blood rise. "Rehabilitation is defined as the act or process of making possible a compatible use for a property through repair, alterations, and additions while preserving those portions or features which convey its historical, cultural, or architectural values." She looked up at him, her square face and broad forehead framed by the Cleopatra cut. "You fail," she said, and turned to leave. Warren followed at her elbow.

"Define 'compatible use'," he demanded.

"I don't have to."

Warren stopped in his tracks, then rushed to catch up. "It's a tobacco warehouse for crying out loud," he said gesturing like a windmill. "You mean to say I could fill the place with carcinogens, but I can't put in tanning beds."

"Iron lungs would, I suppose, convey something of its historical meaning." They were at the exit now. "But not tanning beds."

"What is up with you?" he shouted. Bull was making for her truck. Warren stomped and paced like a baseball manager beside a one-eyed umpire. "What gives you the right?" She produced a business card, tucked it inside his shirt pocket.

"I'm the president of the Darlington Historical Society. It's my way or the highway, Speck-no Pussy."

"My name's Warren."

"Whatever." They were at her truck. Inside the cab was a black German Shepherd the size of Bigfoot. When she opened the door, Warren saw the dog's yellow teeth and its black hair rise in a threatening dark halo, hiding the studded collar around its thick neck.

"I'm opening in five days. And you ain't stopping me." Speck-no gave Bull his best Charles Manson smile. The dog beast began a low growl.

"You're right," she said, shutting the door. "I can't. It'll take a week to get the papers drawn up. But if you do open, you'll be fined. It will cost you big-time. Think about it, Speck-no."

Warren was up on tiptoes, leaning into her window. "Why the hell are you doing this?" The Shepherd's muscles knotted. Its expansive black chest slowly distended. "Why?"

"Because I can," she snarled.

Warren experienced the next second in slow motion: As the giant black Shepherd exploded across the cab toward him, eyes as wide as a shark's, teeth gleaming with slime, Speck-no released a roar that blasted the beast backwards into a simpering furry heap on the floorboard.

The look on Bull's face defied anything Warren had ever seen. Indistinguishable from a lightning strike or the ecstasy of a revelation, her eyes wide in wild disbelief, she whispered in a thick swoon, "Daaaaammmn."

***

Speck-no's Hell

Warren Spector lived the next three days inside his truck. He didn't sleep. He hardly ate. He racked up the miles but saw little of the scenery. He made of Kings Highway and Highway 17 an oval track from Cherry Grove, past Myrtle Beach, down to Garden City, then back up again. He drove these laps like a zombie in a bumper car, his bloodshot eyes seeing nothing. His efforts to channel CP were met with poor reception.

All around him summer was winding down. Fat, strawberry-colored Midwesterners lumbered outside his window, dragging beach towels, chairs, and chubby kids. Dead jellyfish and spent seaweed littered the beach. The humid summer haze turned the afternoon sky gray, and the desert-like wind blew a blanket of stinging sand against the tender calves of the occasional jogger. The smell of dead fish hovered like a toxic cloud over the Cherry Grove Pier.

At Ocean Drive, he stopped for a hotdog. Like an oracle awaiting a prophecy, he looked for a sign, listened for a small voice. None came. At Garden City, he stopped for gas. Darkness had descended. He looked up. Riding the high wind were the sounds of The Wobblers. He parked and followed the music. The band had set up over the water at the end of the pier. The thin crowd called out the titles of songs by dead guys and the hard wind toppled the drummer's cymbal stands. Speck-no ordered a beer he didn't want, one that was too warm to drink by the time it was delivered to him. He dropped the full bottle into a large plastic trashcan and headed back down the pier. To the south were the scattered lights of Pawley's Island.

Nobody in the band had recognized him.

Warren found himself sitting behind the wheel of his truck, parked in the empty Rocket Science lot. Above him, on the sign, he read S n! rf!! A d S ds!!! He lifted the business card from his shirt pocket, read the name, Susan S. Odom, Darlington Historical Society President. He read the sign again, this time aloud, then shifted into gear and headed back to Darlington. All that had once held the scent of gardenias smelled now of rotting shrimp.

Young Warren Spector, who had been born with a dream and the face of a Rottweiler, had decided to kill Susan Bull S. Odom. Maybe he'd get a prison cell beside CP's. Without a dream, doomed to a world that denied him any woman's love, life didn't much seem like living.

Outside the IGA in Darlington, he ran his finger down the torn page of the telephone directory looking for Bull's address. There was no listing. "All I got now," he whispered, "is empty time." He climbed back behind the wheel. If necessary, he'd crisscross the small city until he found her. But first, he'd hit the nightspots. He started with the Little Nashville Club, then circled the Palomino but without luck. Then before he pulled in at The Paradise Lounge, he spotted her pickup. He cruised by to see if her dog was inside. He wasn't. Speck-no parked in the SAV-WAY lot and waited. He'd nail her in the parking lot. In his exhausted, broken heart, one death seemed to equal another.

Warren took a deep breath. His body exhaled for the first time in days. A sense of dark peacefulness rushed in.

When he opened his eyes, he saw Bull's pickup pull out of the lot. He didn't lose sight of her taillights. But she was inside her small brick house by the time he parked on Spain Street, a block away. He waited until her house was dark.

A deluxe doghouse occupied the back corner of the fenced yard. But there was no sign of the dog. He delicately opened the chain-link gate, crept inside and crouched under a window with his back against the warm brick. He could wait. Susan S. Odom would put the dog out for the night, and then Warren Spector would put Susan out to pasture.

When Speck-no heard Bull's voice from inside the bedroom above him, he held his breath. He didn't move. He couldn't make out anything she was saying or who she was saying it to. It didn't sound much like talking. But whatever it was was so familiar that for a moment he experienced something like Déjà vu. Then he knew. He'd heard those primal sounds before, behind the Wobblers' dressing room door. The little cries began to rise in pitch. The breathless gasps were audible now. There was no doubt.

A debilitating fatigue settled over him. Not only was he denied the satisfaction of revenge for losing Speck-Some Beach, he was submitted to the shame of knowing that even Bull could get laid. He sat with his face in his hands until Susan S. Odom's cries turned into little breathy squeals. Then he slowly rose, covered his ears, and headed back to his truck.

The next morning, Warren Spector woke to the thunderous sounds of NASCAR engines. He sat up in his truck and rubbed the sleep from his eyes. It was Labor Day at Speck-Some Beach. Three miles away, thousands of race fans from all over the country waited for the green flag. Behind him, Warren heard the sound of a horn and watched as a

Cadillac pulling a fifteen-foot trailer entered the Speck-Some lot. On the trailer lay a construction resembling a small tower. The smoked window on the driver's side of the Cadillac silently descended. CP sat at the wheel.

"Howdy, Bo. I got a present for you."

Speck-no opened the rear bay door and CP backed the trailer inside.

"Where'd you get this thing?" Speck-no said.

"It's a gift, to you. Don't you worry where it came from."

It was a wooden lifeguard stand uprooted from somewhere on the Grand Strand. "Call it community service from a guy out on bail," CP said.

"The two of us are never gonna get this baby up," said Speck-no. "It's eighteen feet tall." He studied its dimensions, its construction. "Six hundred and twenty-five pounds."

"WHAD HE SAY?" The voice at 150 decibels was Dirk's. Standing beside her in identical black Harley leather was Tasha. The two smiling women raised their arms and flexed their biceps.

***

Speck-no's Beach

Speck-no was not a poet. He was a former roadie for a frat band. He looked at the world around him and made sense of it as best he could, describing to himself what he saw with the words he had for doing it. His was the language of light and sound, and he didn't think of the two as separate; both were waves. He knew the connection between a blue light and a blue note. He could hear a sound and call it brown or time a lighting effect to simulate a cymbal crash. He could hear a rainbow. This didn't make him a poet, but it did give him a perspective. A good life, like a great song, shouldn't be measured in time. You could go from the beginning of a life to its end and never live a single day. Speck-Some Beach might live but a day, but that day would be Speck-no's.

At midnight, Warren Spector sat atop the lifeguard stand, head back, eyes closed. He wore the Harley tank top Dirk had given him, the Harley baseball cap from Tasha, and CP's gift, the sunglasses that had rested for thirty years on the face of a mannequin in the lobby of Rocket Science. The reflected heat from the tanning beds radiated around him. The sound and smell of the Atlantic mingled with the scent of suntan lotion and drifted on the soft currents. Below, the music of The Wobblers surfaced from time to time over the noise of the crowd. Warren was bathing in the moment.

"WE GODDA BE HEADIN' OUT," Dirk said. Speck-no's eyes flew open. He stood. Dirk motioned. "No, keep your seat. We gotta head out. Somebody took over our campsite." She smiled.

"Thanks for the good time," Tasha said. "I didn't think anything could lift me from the depths of a Jeff Gordon victory." They held hands and walked away, melting into the crowd.

Speck-Some Beach was packed. Barely clad women and men swarmed around the three bars, their bodies so close that some carried their beers above their head like a victory salute. The trophy women occupied the patio tables in twos or threes. A steady stream of men circled each table, some just cruising, others casting their lines, testing their bait. Outside the facades of The Galleon, The Bowery, The Showhouse, and other Myrtle Beach clubs, beautiful women stood in line for the tanning beds, sipping their fruity drinks and sizing up the competition. The electric excitement of romantic anticipation buzzed and crackled. Pheromones choked the air. Testosterone waves and estrogen clouds set off a storm of sexual lightning.

Speck-no watched as a sea of men at the far end of the boardwalk parted and a dozen silicon inspired lap dancers from The Trophy Club glided toward the first bar. The troops fell in behind them like midgets leaving the Emerald City. In their wake, Speck-no spotted a dark figure in bulky camouflaged coveralls and wearing combat boots.

Susan S. Odom. Bull.

Warren watched her disappear behind The Alabama Theater. He folded his sunglasses, slid them into his pocket, and climbed down from the lifeguard stand. He'd never hit a woman. He'd spent his life loving them from afar. But he had never been so close to a dream before either, and the loss of the one seemed to justify the crime of the other. If he could find her, he wouldn't hit her, but he would sure as hell escort Bull out of his club. He made his way toward her, dodging and weaving past the thinly clad, scanning for the over-sized coveralls, looking down for the boots. He felt the muscles in his forearms tighten, his stomach turn over. He began pushing his way through.

Then, from the opposite end of the beach, he heard The Wobblers begin their minor hit, If You Ain't Here After What I'm Here After, You'll Be Here After I'm Gone. The chorus of voices began at the front of the stage and then surged back toward Warren like a tidal wave. Every face turned as the voices rose in unison, stranger embraced stranger, and smiles like whitecaps rushed forward then back again across the crowd. Warren stopped. This was a moment of his creation.

Suddenly overcome by tenderness and longing, he turned and made his way back to his lifeguard stand. He sat high above the crowd as closing time neared, looking at one lovely woman then another, whispering to himself, "Life preservers, life boats, life lines." Susan S. Odom disappeared from his mind.

At 1:45 the sax player for The Wobblers shouted, "Last call for alcohol!" At 2:15, he announced that in five minutes the hounds would be released to empty the place. At 2:30, Speck-no stood high atop the towering lifeguard stand and put on a display of K-9 fury that left the remaining drunks slack-jawed and wide-eyed. When he was done, the remaining patrons turned and gave him an ovation. "Daaaaaaammmmmn," they all murmured. Then they slowly and obediently waltzed out the exits.

It was nearly four in the morning when the servers cashed out and the bartenders cleaned up. They were all too exhausted to talk. In twos and threes, they smiled at Speck-no, tossed up a tired salute and headed for the door. The beach was quiet, except for the pre-recorded sounds of surf and the occasional squawk of a gull.

Warren sat alone, looking out over Speck-Some Beach, not thinking about tomorrow—the notices on the door, the chain, and padlock. Not really thinking at all. He embraced a feeling, the warm sensation that lingered in the empty warehouse like a song inside his head. He thought: Lovers found one another here tonight. Bodies radiated with heat. Hearts opened. The laws of probability say that at least one of those, maybe more, will be a true and lasting love.

Speck-no sat for a very long time. Then he climbed down slowly and drifted toward the control panels. He did not hurry. Instead, his movements were like a slow dance as he turned and looked and paused and then spread his arms to this world of romance. Near the spot where he and Dirk and Tasha had slept six months earlier, Warren Spector threw the electrical switches, and the sun, the surf, and the suds disappeared into silent darkness. He dug his keys from his pocket. He felt for the door. Then he stopped.

He faced the dark beach, and from the very bottom of him came a cry that filled the black emptiness around him. That lonesome howl passed above the clouds, beyond the length of his beach, and circled to him.

He lifted his hand like a blind man and held the door.

A second voice echoed from the darkness. Warren stopped. "Say it again," the soft voice whispered. He stepped into the blackness, listening for the phantom voice. "Again." The small voice seemed to come from everywhere.

Standing in the vastness of deep empty space, Warren closed his eyes, held his breath.

A spontaneous wail rose from his depths, coalesced into a single note of desire and despair, then rushed out of him.

"Oh, yes," responded the voice.

"Red wine," said Warren. "Your voice is the color of red wine."

"And chocolate. Once more," the wine voice pleaded.

Warren's arms went out before him, and now with control and conviction his voice rose slowly to a pitch that could only be called music. It was the soulful sound of primeval passion and sorrow, a Percy Sledge kind of music.

"Here," she said in a crooning whisper, so close he could feel its heat upon his ear.

In the total blindness of this universe, invisible fingers touched, then lifted his hand. Straight, long hair cascaded over and between his fingers. Slowly, she coaxed his hand down the length of her neck. She pressed his fingertips around a zipper above her breasts, then gently guided his hand downward. His palms inched inside the loose fabric, over her thin, smooth shoulders. Tender passion radiated from her bare skin, from her hands upon his face, from her beating heart against his.

They kissed, just once. Then Warren held her in his arms. Eyes closed, he listened to their synchronous breathing, that slow in and out, and felt the gentle sway of their bodies like the motion of an eternal tide.

END

CPSIA information can be obtained at www.ICGtesting.com
Printed in the USA
LVOW082333090512

281008LV00002B/2/P